Feeling isolated and alone, Jenni seeks comfort with her special tree. Through a magical twist she slips back in time to Mesolithic Britain. There, amongst people who teach her respect and a deep spiritual connection to the natural world, she finally finds friendship. However, not everyone in the group is pleased to accept her and it isn't long before Jenni is forced into a situation where she has to rely on her wits and newly acquired skills to survive. Will she ever make it back to the future? And what is her special connection with the revered Elder Druantia?

Pam C Golden's exciting timeslip novel was inspired by her love of nature, magic and a fascination with the ancient past.

Pam C Golden had a happy childhood full of love and books which led her to study teaching. Once she had finished her education, she found her wings and flew. After many adventures around the world, she finally met her husband and they settled down in Yorkshire, where their son was born. Pam has always had a vivid imagination and started writing her first children's novel when she was nine. Although that was never completed, she is now realising her life-long ambition to become a children's writer.

Other books by Pam C Golden

TO BE HUMAN IS AN HONOUR
a memoir

Find out more about Pam and her books
on her website at gentlepresspublishing.co.uk

or

Follow her on Instagram, Twitter and Facebook

Pam C Golden

Artwork for cover image
created by
Harry J Davies

Published
by

GENTLE PRESS

GENTLE PRESS

Published by Gentle Press Publications

First published 2020

ISBN 978-1-9163301-0-8

Dedication

To the indigenous people of Earth
who have known and understood plant life
since the beginning of Time
and to everyone who has ever stood under
a tree and marvelled at its beauty.

PART ONE
Difficult Relationships

CHAPTER 1
The Oak Arch

"I'm fed up of being different. Leave me alone!" banging the door shut, I storm off, unaware of the slow tear that trickles down my mum's face.

A strand of hair gets in my eyes so I brush it angrily aside. 'Red arrows' flick round my head. My hair ribbon, ineffectual as ever, hangs limply down my back. Life is so unfair. No matter what I say to Mum, nothing seems to get through. The argument goes round and round my head, as I stamp up the path.

"You don't understand. I'm left out at school. They all think I'm odd. Zari and Mina laugh at me, Alex and her friends don't understand why I don't know anything about make-up. I've nothing to talk about. It's all because you won't let me have a tablet or phone, never mind a telly. It's not fair."

"Believe me, one day you will thank me for not filling your head with technological nonsense," is always her reply.

I could never imagine when that day will come. Even my aunt has tried to stand up for me, telling her it's cruel, but she got nowhere.

"It limits your mind and imagination. I never had these things as a child. I grew to be really grateful. We're better off without it all." Mum conveniently forgets she was born in the Stone Age.

A hot feeling of shame floods through, as I remember earlier when Zari and Mina shut the door in my face. Desperate to get the attention of the new boy, Jonti, they kept flicking their hair back and giggling every time he went past, pretending they didn't hear me trying to join them. Tears prick behind my eyes. It had only got worse. Sitting by the sad little beech tree in the playground, I'd tried to make myself invisible and imagine a world where people cared about each other and the world around them. The tree had rustled its leaves in sympathy but Kenzo and his mates saw me all alone and had dive bombed me, calling me names.

I brush the tears away with my sleeve and sniff, grateful there are no dog walkers around. As always, climbing the hill helps my head to clear. By the time I reach the top road, I'm feeling a bit better. Green mossy walls glow under the sun, highlighting the uneven shapes of the stones. Fields of quietly grazing sheep spread out on either side. I begin to slow down. I love it up here. Taking deeper breaths, the cool air fills my lungs. On the opposite side, the hills loom gently against the blue sky. The valley below has become a mere dip in the landscape, so I can pretend it isn't there; and with it, school and all the nastiness it holds.

I try so hard to make friends but nothing seems to work. I wish I knew what to do. It's all Mum's fault making me so different. At least no one from school ever comes this way; it's like my own private world.

Turning off the road I head down the path leading into the woods. Sunlight filters through the leaves, the birds include me in their songs, my feet can feel the softer earth and it all makes me feel calmer. Up ahead, I can see my favourite spot; two oak trees creating an arch over the path. I used to love coming here with Mum when I was little. We'd imagine the leafy gateway could be a portal to different worlds. I miss those days. Looking up at the shades of green above, I can see all the delicate veins in each leaf highlighted by the sun.

The tree stands solid and comfortable. Leaning into it, I put my head between a side branch and the main trunk. The cool limbs feel very soothing so I close my eyes for a moment. As always, a few seconds later, a tiny breeze appears from nowhere, rustling the leaves. It feels as if the tree is saying hello.

A very deep sigh slips out, as I snuggle closer into the trunk. Normally I'd look around to check no one can see me; the odd walker or cyclist sometimes uses this path, but today I don't care. The tree feels so comfortable. I'm a part of it and it is a part of me.

I look up, squinting against the bright, sun-filtered green. Is it my imagination or is the green light moving? A hazy softness surrounds me, while the light seems to be swirling in and out of my body. A strange buzzing starts to fill every part of me, as if hundreds of tiny, but cosy bees are bursting out. It's very strange, but it doesn't feel bad. The branches of the tree start to spin an arm-like web of support as I sway backwards and forwards with the strange sound. Worries gone, I snuggle closer in to the warm, welcoming glow.

With my eyes firmly shut, the tree seems to be

wrapping itself around me, as the tiny breeze turns into a stronger wind. I lean closer into the security of the trunk. The internal buzzing vibrates more and more, the rustling from the leaves grows louder and louder, and soon I can't tell what's inside or outside of me.

Keeping my eyes tightly shut, I suddenly start to spin, as if I'm in a whirlpool. I need to look. I need to see what's going on. Flicking my eyelids open for a second is enough. Green lights of every shade and depth flash passed in swirls. Is this what it's like to faint? Snapping my eyes shut I take several deep breaths and lean more into the body of the tree to try and steady myself. As I breathe, it feels as if a green light is permeating every pore. Time itself seems to stop. I have no idea how long I have been here.

CHAPTER 2
Where in the World?

Finally, the wind dies away, the buzzing quietens down and my head starts to stop spinning. Keeping my eyes closed, I stand very quietly, trying to work out what just happened. A smell fills my senses, unlike anything I've ever smelled before; a sort of rich, earthy scent mingled with intense green growth.

Suddenly I hear a walker coming. Normally I'd move away quickly from the tree and pretend to be looking at a squirrel or something. But I feel so dizzy. I don't think I can trust myself to leave the tree trunk and not fall over. Then I remember something I read once about people in the rainforest who blend themselves into the trees, staying very still, so other people can't see them. It's like they become invisible. I'm invisible to most people anyway, so I'm sure I can manage it.

The footsteps are coming closer. With every bit of effort, I imagine myself as part of the tree, blending into the trunk, the bark covering me, still as a statue. The footsteps are louder now, leaves crunching underfoot, the odd twig snapping. The footsteps stop. I hear breathing. I daren't open my eyes. Please, please don't let me be seen.

"Well it's a good try, but you still need more practice. You've a way to go yet."

My eyes snap open. Before me stands a healthy looking boy, about my age; but there's something different about him. Something I can't quite put my finger on. His brown eyes are looking at me in a quizzical way while dark, curly hair frames his serious face. His wiry body is slim but athletic looking; I can tell there is hidden strength in those muscles. His clothes, yes, they're very strange, but it's something else. A glow seemed to emanate from all around him and a smell of fresh earth and leaves and... what is it? He seems 'more than alive' is the only way I can express it.

"Oh! I thought you were my sister. Where have you come from? I thought I knew everyone round here." His voice is pleasant but wary.

This is my special place. Where has he appeared from and who does he think he is? "I might say the same to you. I've never seen you round here before."

I try to stare him out and he does the same to me. Then I notice his clothes. He's not wearing trousers or jeans but a long sort of shift and his feet are bare. That must be where the leaf smell comes from; his clothes look as if they're made out of them, carefully woven together. They can't be. The boy suddenly speaks, echoing my thoughts.

"You look different..." he starts.

That's it. He's asked for it now. I launch into full attack, "Well so do you! I suppose you're off to a party or something. Of course *I* won't be invited to anything like that because no one wants to be bothered with me. I'm the one who's always different. I'm never going to fit in. You wouldn't either if you weren't allowed a phone or even a television." I stop. What am I thinking of letting this strange boy know how I feel? Annoying tears start to blur everything and I turn away quickly so he can't see.

"What are you talking about? What's a fone and what's a tel'vision?" he asks.

Oh he's really laughing at me now. "Stop making fun of me!" I yell. "I've hardly met you and you're being mean. Leave me alone!"

I stumble away trying to put a distance between us. I can hear him calling me to wait. I'm not listening. I start to run, 'cloudy bubbles' forming round my head. Floundering blindly through the woods, my ankle catches in something and I fall over. Landing on my bottom, I feel stupid and angry. All I can think of is that he's going to laugh at me even more now. I look down. A creeper has somehow twisted itself around my leg. Struggling to get up, a burning sensation sears through my ankle. I collapse back. He reaches me as I'm trying to stand again. I can't help it. I gasp in pain.

"Are you alright?" he asks.

"No!" I shout. "Isn't it obvious?" He eyes me up as if he's making a decision.

"Wait there," he states quietly, "I'll get help."

"Well, it's not as if I can go anywhere," I mutter.

In the next moment I'm alone. It hurts. A lot. Trying not to cry, I edge my foot into a more comfortable position. Nearby is a fallen log. I remember when Mum sprained her ankle she had to keep it raised up. I wonder if that will help?

Gradually inching my leg across, I lift it onto the log and lean back on my elbows. Taking a few deep breaths seems to relieve the pain a little. As I do so, I look up into the branches above. Something's not quite right. The trees seem to be closer together than normal. I shift over to get a better look but the slight movement causes a shooting pain to race up my leg. Gasping, I try to focus on the sky. Earlier it was blue and the sun was shining; now it's cloudy but the air seems clearer and more vibrant, as if the air itself was awake. "Stop being silly," I tell myself. "How can the air be alive?"

Suddenly, I hear footsteps returning. Hurriedly pushing myself back up, I see two tall and very beautiful women walking alongside the boy. Long tunics, similar to his, gracefully adorn their bodies; decorated with leaves in beautiful patterns and shapes. The women look as if they are related, with soft, brown skin and long hair, falling in black wavy curls down their backs. As they move, an agile vitality emanates from them. One has gentle, brown eyes reminding me of Mum; while the other has stunningly blue eyes which seem to pierce far beyond the surrounding trees to a magical place that no one else could see.

Their smiles are dazzling. Soft voices tell me to relax. They gently lift me up on to the crook of a nearby tree. Standing either side, holding the palm of their hands towards my throbbing ankle, I feel warmth flood through me, like I've never felt before. All at once, I feel happy, contented and safe. Suddenly I realise that my ankle isn't hurting.

"What have you done?"

"We've healed you," the blue-eyed woman replies,

as if it's totally normal. "The children are always falling and needing mending, it's part of growing up." They lift me down and watch while I gingerly test my ankle.

"It really is better!" I am amazed.

"Rhodri told us to come quickly," the other woman continues, "but we didn't realise it was for a stranger. You are very welcome. Please stay as long as you like and share with us in our Living."

Although in my head I'm thinking this is too weird to be happening and I shouldn't trust strangers, my instincts are telling me the complete opposite. I feel comfortable and relaxed with these people.

"I can't stop long," I reply, to cover myself. "My mum will wonder where I am."

"Where do you live?" Rhodri asks.

"Halfway down the hill, a bit further on, beyond the end of the path," I turn round to point out the route to my house but the whole landscape has changed. "Where is it?" I demand.

For the first time, I look around at exactly where I am. I can see my oak tree arch but that's all. Gone are the stone walls, gone the sheep in the green fields beyond; gone the path, mud worn with walkers and cyclists.

Vibrant green trees stand around as far as I can see and sunlight filters through the branches, dappling the floor with glowing greens and yellows. The rich air seems full of bird song and animals are chattering in the trees with some running across the soft, leaf deep carpet beneath us.

"Where am I?" I whisper.
"You are in the Land, where else would you be?"
"But … my home, my mum … where's it all gone?"
"We don't understand you, this is all there is. Is your mum in the next Living?"
"What do you mean, next living? Of course my mum's living. What's happened?"

All at once I start to feel panic welling up inside. This place is all very beautiful but it's so far beyond anything I've ever known. Everything familiar has gone. 'Black and white arrows' point in on me, my mind feels all muddled and I start to run towards the only recognisable thing in this strange and intense landscape.

The oak tree arch looms ahead. I pick up my pace, desperate for some normality. From nowhere a root appears and my foot catches against it. Vaguely registering "Not again," I am falling through the air until my forehead smashes with a sickening thud into the trunk. Pain sears through my brain and everything goes black.

CHAPTER 3
Time before Time

"She will recover soon."
"Why are her clothes so different?"
"I am sure all will be revealed as the sun moves across the sky."
"She needs rest."
Snatches of conversation drift in and around me. I feel very comfortable and snuggle further down in bed. The words don't make much sense but why would they? I'm dreaming. Nothing makes sense in a dream. I'll give myself a few more minutes and then I'll get up for school. I drift off again. Floating blissfully on a bed of soft moss covered in leaves, I edge my sluggish mind into wakefulness.

Gradually opening my eyes, the first thing I notice is that I am under a greenish yellow canopy. With a shock, I realise I'm not at home in bed. Moving my hands, I discover the bed of leaves and moss is a reality. Turning, I see several kind-looking people sitting nearby, watching me with care and concern on their faces. An older person, with years of love in her wrinkles, is nearest.
"How are you feeling?" she asks.
"I'm not sure," I reply.

Looking up, I recognise two of the women.
"I remember you. I hurt myself. You came and healed my ankle. What happened next?"
"We saw 'lots of arrows' around you, waves of a strange feeling came over us and you ran. Before

we knew it, you'd tripped, flown towards a tree trunk, hit your head and fallen. We went to help, but knew we needed to bring you to our Living. A head injury has to be healed by an Elder," one of the women replies.

I look up at the wise and caring face gazing at me with calm, loving eyes. "You must be an Elder. What's going on? Where am I? What's happened to me?"

"You are still recovering. Try not to distress yourself. When you fell, our first task was to heal you. While you were sleeping and recovering, we realised there was something special about you. You are a mystery; your clothes, your looks, all tell of a story very different from ours. As it is beyond anything in my own experience, I decided to seek advice from the Place of Learning."

The Elder pauses, allowing her words to sink in. "There I discovered something astounding. You are from another Time." I look at her carefully. Not sure what to believe, I keep quiet. She seems a good person; she doesn't look like she'd lie to me. But surely she can't believe that? I stay very still and decide to play along for now.

The woman continues. "I was told that your world is far, far beyond our Living. An unbelievable passage of suns will take place before the world in which you come from is born. For some reason, not yet clear, you have slipped from your world into ours. You will be worried about your family but you have no need. They won't know you have gone. When you are ready to return, no time will have passed in your world."

She must be joking. No, this can't be true. Yet...those deep, brown, kindly eyes, they would never lie. She obviously believes it. Is she some sort of a nutter? But she doesn't look like one. Could there be something in it? Do I have any choice other than to go along with it? It certainly looks very different from the world I know. What if I have slipped in time? Is it so impossible? I'm used to being odd and different; why not be completely so, by being in another era?

Understanding and sympathy is reflected back to me in the eyes of the others. "I know this is hard for you. It is hard for us too. For now, you need to rest and recover. Try to enjoy being with us, something very special is happening here. " Smiling a beautiful smile, the Elder fades gently away, leaving me looking at the two younger women in a daze.

"I'm finding this a bit hard to believe," I confide. "It's a lot to think about."

"Don't worry. For now you need to rest, as Druantia said. I'm sure all will become clear. Try to sleep, we are nearby," they tell me.

My head is swimming with questions, but a wave of exhaustion pushes me into oblivion.

I'm not sure how long I've been asleep. Gently rising into a wakeful state, I blink and start to take in my surroundings again. Above me a canopy of leaves interlock forming a natural shelter from the elements. Sunlight is peeking through the odd gap, shafting lines of light to the floor around me. Undulating birdsong fills the sky, while closer by I can hear lots of little rustling sounds. Somewhere in the far distance I think I can pick out the murmuring of voices. An intensely green, leafy smell permeates the air. Looking down, the floor seems to be made of tightly cropped grass. I'm encircled by closely interwoven branches of hawthorn; with an opening, which has grown into an archway.

Through this opening I notice a slightly familiar face looking in at me. It's the boy I met when I entered this strange world.

He approaches cautiously, "How are you?" he asks warily.

"Much better," I answer. He looks a bit nervous so I add, "Thank you."

The boy's face relaxes a little. "Well, the Elders have told me to look after you, since I brought you here. I'm glad to hear you're feeling better. My name's Rhodri by the way."

"Mine's Jenni." I feel like saying that he doesn't have to stay if it is too much effort but I bite my tongue and keep quiet for a change. There's an awkward pause. I fish around trying to think of something to say. Finally I say, "Do you live nearby? Is your house close to here?"

Rhodri seems to be thinking carefully about how to answer. "I don't quite know what you mean by house," he starts cautiously, "we all spend our rest time in the Rest Space; like this, only bigger. This is the Healing Space; you have been allowed to sleep here to recover, but tonight you can join us, if you are well enough."

"So you all live outside? What about when it

rains?"
The boy seems to relax a bit, "Oh it doesn't rain so much and when it does, we enjoy it. It's a time to have a rain wash. I love rain days." Then he looks at me shyly, "Can I ask you something? What are those things made of that you're wearing?"
"My jeans and T-shirt? They're made of cotton. Don't you have cloth like it?"
"No. How's it made?"

I start to explain, as far as I know, how cloth is woven in a factory and stitched by a machine into the things I'm wearing. Rhodri looks horrified.
"You mean they do the same thing all day, every day? Why don't other people help-share with them?"
I try to describe how it works but the more I speak, the more genuinely confused Rhodri appears to be.

I'm beginning to think I really must have travelled back in time. How else can this boy, his clothes, his so-called home and his reactions be explained? I begin to realise this is going to be difficult. Rhodri's life seems very different from mine; if I really have arrived in the distant past, then the future is so complex and crazy in comparison. Sighing to myself, I realise that travelling back in time hasn't stopped my usual problem. Although trying really hard to get on with him, everything I say seems to be illuminating how far apart we are. There is one slight difference; at least he isn't running away from me... yet. Feeling desperate to cling to this slither of friendship, I change the subject, "Tell me more about your world."

As he talks about familiar things, I'm happy to see him starting to relax more. Rhodri tells me how they gather food from the forest. Everything is based on the trees. The trees give them their life. They eat the leaves; he likes the sweet lime and nutty hawthorn ones best. They gather fruits and berries, dig up roots and every so often they eat meat from an animal or fish from a river. He tells me about their clothes; how the hunters bring home smooth skins, which the people in the Living make into tunics.

"Why do they look as if they are made out of leaves?" I ask.

"We all enjoy making the tunics look special in our own way. We choose a variety of leaves and stitch them on to the skins. Each of us likes to create our own individual patterns and colours. It's very satisfying when you've made a new pattern that makes you happy."

As we have been talking the sunbeams start to slant at a lower angle through the leaves and the sunlight is beginning to fade. I snatch a glance at Rhodri's face; his expression seems softer than earlier. Maybe, just maybe, I haven't done too badly? The boy, however, seems keen to get away. "Are you ready to come and meet the others?" he asks.

Feeling a little nervous, I wonder if I have any choice in the matter. I'd rather stay longer in this safe place but he looks impatient to go. Slowly, I step through the hawthorn arch. All around us, the trees stand; giving me the feeling that they are almost alive in a human way. As I follow Rhodri, this feeling intensifies. I could swear the branches actually move to let us pass, while the leaves rattle in a sudden gust of wind. It reminds me of being with my favourite oak tree, but all the trees are doing it.

After a short while, Rhodri gestures to an arch of lime, similar to the arch we've just left. "Here we are; you go first." Wishing the ground would swallow me up; I step cautiously into the archway.

There I stop. A group of beautiful looking people, all dressed like Rhodri, are sitting around on the mossy rocks and floor. Gentle laughter and chatter flow around while small children play among them, giggling at each other and placing little stones in some sort of game. One or two people are engaged in what looks like carving, other people seem to be sewing, while others are relaxing and chatting. A fire glows in the middle, its soft light flickering and dancing in the gentle flames.

Across the space, I recognise the two women who helped me. They look up and smile. Up above I notice the branches have been woven into a frame, while dusk lends softness to the scene, blending the edges of all the shapes.

Beautiful as it is, the sight isn't what has stopped me. It's the feeling. A wave of love and calm sweeps through and cradles me. It's much stronger than before, when the women had come to help. I feel accepted in a way I've always longed to be.

Feeling very self-conscious, I blink hard, fighting back the tears.

CHAPTER 4
Green Life

"Hi, are you Rhodri's friend?" a chirpy voice pipes up.

A short, stocky girl, probably a couple of years younger than me, is looking at me with kind, brown eyes. Dark hair tumbles around her face in unruly curls. With the word 'friend' echoing in my head, I turn to her.

"I'm his sister, Adara. Everyone's been talking about you." Adara's warmth draws me into the group. Smiles radiate from every face as they all acknowledge my presence. The nervousness in my tummy begins to go away, as Adara proudly introduces me. Out of the corner of my eye, I notice Rhodri looking relieved as he melts back into the group.

With a slight sense of panic, I start to worry about remembering all their names. I've already forgotten most of them. When we are part way round the group, another child comes in through the arch; a girl with a sharp face looks me up and down. She's slim and wiry, looking as if she exists on a lot of nervous energy. Her sinewy arms hang tensely by her side. I don't like the look of her. She may be thin but she looks very strong. I decide it wouldn't be a good idea to cross her. She moves across the group and I feel a warning prickle, as her eyes settle on me.

"So, this is the stranger," the grating voice says,

then she abruptly turns away. I shrink back against a rock wanting to disappear. A small hand slips into mine and I look down to see Adara, "Don't mind Froni, she often says things sharply but no one takes any notice." I look at the little girl gratefully. It's a new feeling, someone sticking up for me. I see Rhodri smiling across at his sister and an unexplained warm glow spreads inside.

As darkness falls, I lie on a bed of moss and leaves, with Adara on one side and Rhodri on the other. The two names I can remember from the introductions belong to the beautiful women who rescued me. Adienna, the woman with the stunning blue eyes is Rhodri and Adara's mother and Cara, her kind brown-eyed sister. Wondering what tomorrow will bring and whether I should worry about the warning prickle, I drift off into sleep.

Birdsong deafens me, as the fresh morning light filters through the canopy. Stretching and wriggling, I roll over and sit up. All around people are emerging from their dreams. Adienna comes across, glowing with smiles. "How are you feeling now our little, broken one? Are you feeling hungry?" Now she's mentioned food, I suddenly realise how hungry I am.

"Come. I'll show you how we eat." Following her, I find myself in a clearing among the trees. Rhodri skips off to collect his own food and looks quite happy not to have to be bothered by me. I try not to notice.

"Now, sit still and wait," Adienna tells me. As we sit, an intense feeling of love washes through me and I realise it's coming from Adienna. I feel as if I would do anything for this woman; the feeling is so strong. Looking around, I notice a rustling in the trees above us. Scurrying sounds and tiny chattering noises can be heard overhead. The lime tree we're sitting under starts dropping some of its young leaves. Wide ovals of green with a point at one end start tumbling into my lap. Adienna pops one in her mouth and chews. "Go on," she urges "eat." Gingerly I put one in my mouth and chew it round. It's juicy, with a hint of sweetness and isn't as bad as I thought it would be. I try another one.

Chewing the leaves, I notice a group of red squirrels. I wonder if they are the creatures in the trees above us. Scared of frightening them, I sit very still. I watch as they run up to Adienna and I'm amazed to see them drop some hazelnuts in her lap. They run back to a pile hidden beyond my sight and return with more.

"Why do they do it?" I ask. "Don't they want to keep them for themselves?"

Adienna smiles and explains that the little creatures love to work with humans. "We help them, give them love and they help us. While they are in our area, they know they are safe from the bigger creatures who kill and harm them. They know we protect them. In exchange, they share their hoard of nuts, which they gather in the golden leaf time. They feel our love and want to give love back. This is their way."

"Don't they need all the nuts for their own food?"

"No, they always gather much more than they can eat themselves and are happy to share."

I think about my future life and how differently people think about animals. Some people adore their animals and are kind to them, but not everyone. I remember an assembly at school where a visitor talked about the harm done to all sorts of creatures. The woman was trying to raise funds for a charity and I remember being very upset by what she told us. Even Zari had tears in her eyes.

I suddenly realise that Adienna is talking to me. "Have you had enough to eat?"
Although we've only had a few leaves and nuts, each leaf and nut seemed so full of vibrant energy; I don't feel hungry any more.

"I'm fine thank you." I don't quite know how to put the next question but I'm very grateful it's the woman, not her son I'm asking.
"Um, this is a bit embarrassing but where do I go to the toilet? I managed an emergency wee yesterday when no one was looking but I'm not sure where the toilets are. "

Adienna gives me a strange look and shakes her head in confusion. Then I realise that she doesn't know the word toilet. Burning up with embarrassment, I go through a series of gestures and mimes, until light suddenly illuminates Adienna's eyes. "Oh of course," she smiles. She then explains about the areas outside the main Rest Space where everyone goes. "We never go near sleeping areas or sitting places. Leaves and moss are used to clean ourselves and then we cover it over with more leaves. When you see an area with disturbed leaves, you know what's there and never to sit or sleep near it. If it is fairly fresh then the flies will warn you. Our little friends are very good at that."

"But how do I wash my hands afterwards?" So far I've not seen any water and I'm wondering where I can find a drink. "Use moss first; which cleans your hands so they are tingling and spotless. Then we'll go to the water."

Using moss and leaves isn't half as bad as I thought it would be, in fact it feels rather pleasant when I realise it will all be recycled by nature with no pollution. As some slugs head in the direction of my whiffy poo, I realise that these detested creatures are actually nature's cleaners.

Adienna appears like magic, as I finish. "Are you ready?" she smiles. Wandering together through the trees, I can hardly believe what's happening to me. Was it only the day before yesterday when I was worrying so much about school and friendships?

Soon I can hear the sound of a waterfall. As we emerge from the dense forest growth, large boulders and rocky outcrops mark the space where the water tumbles. Cascading from a high ledge above us, is the clearest, most sparkling pure water that I've ever seen. Drops spin out from the main body, catching the sun and glistening like diamonds. A sudden thirst overwhelms me and I move forward, desperate to plunge into the delicious pool to drink and wash. A strong arm grabs me and holds me back. I look up at Adienna full of shock and surprise.

"We do not treat water in this way," her voice is strong and firm, unlike the gentle person I thought

I knew. “It is too precious.”

“Sit here,” she commands. Sitting on a rock overlooking the tantalisingly cool and beautiful pool, she explains how everyone treats the water.

“Water is the source of everything. She is our life. If we treat her badly we become very sick and die. It is vital we pray to the Water Goddess and offer love before we ask to receive her bounty. We never put our bodies into the river or pools. If we do it’ll make the water bad for other people and later on for us. All the people have agreed on this. We respect the water and keep her pure. I will show you how we do it.”

I watch, with my mouth drying up, as Adienna goes to the water’s edge. As she stands there, I again feel the waves of love I experienced with the squirrels and trees earlier. This time she’s sending it into the water. I’m not sure if it’s my imagination or not but the water definitely seems to flash and sparkle more. Then an amazing thing happens. There’s a rock on the bank, close to the waterfall, with several hollows in the top. The water in the waterfall starts to swing across until it fills the hollows and then it swings back again.

It reminds me of an experiment at school, which fascinated me. We’d been learning about static electricity. The teacher gave us all a comb and told us to comb our hair lots of times and then hold the comb towards a trickle of water coming out of the tap. The stream of water moved towards the comb. I can’t remember why it happened but I know it’s something to do with positive and negative electrons. I wonder if Adienna uses a similar force to move the waterfall.

I look up. My friend's mother is beckoning me to follow. As we reach the hollows in the rock, Adienna speaks. "Gently blow on the surface to clear a space of pure water, then suck it up through your lips. Watch me." I watch, fascinated, as Adienna blows gently on the water, then purses her lips and expertly sucks in the precious liquid. I follow, relishing the cool, delicious liquid as it surges down my dry throat. I drink and drink. Never have I drunk water quite like it. Or any drink to be honest.

Further across from the drinking hollows is a deeper indentation full of water. Adienna scoops some of this with her hand then washes her hands away from the rock, so the dirty water lands on the earth below, not back in the hollow. I follow her example again. It feels so good to feel the silky substance flow over my hands. After managing to splash my face, we walk back to the Living Space feeling wonderfully refreshed.

Adara comes running up, with her brother following behind.

"Oh there you are," she exclaims, her dark curls bouncing round her face, "we've been looking everywhere for you."

"I've been showing our friend how we eat and drink," replies their mother. "Now you need to help her practice."

CHAPTER 5
Froni

Initially, I have to rely on the others in the group for food but the day comes when my first squirrel helper approaches. Waves of gratitude and affection towards this little creature flow from me, forming 'soft pink cloud' shapes. He responds by dropping some precious nuts into my lap. His bushy red tail flicks up as he darts back to his nut store. I sit transfixed. I've done it!

The following days become almost dreamlike. I feel so happy being included by this friendly and easy going sister and brother. Rhodri gradually seems more relaxed in my presence, even though I keep catching him staring at my skin and clothes when he thinks I'm not looking. Occasionally a cheeky grin flashes across his features, transforming his normally serious face. Sometimes it's even directed at me, and when it is, I feel a glow of unfamiliar warmth.

The only time I feel uncomfortable is when Froni wanders past. Glaring at me, she sends waves of hatred in my direction until Adara or Rhodri catch her at it and then she scurries away. I try hard not to let these looks bother me, but they niggle at the back of my mind. Eventually, plucking up my courage I ask, "What's Froni got against me? Every time I try to smile at her, she scowls. What's her problem?"

Rhodri, who's chewing on some gum, looks at me

seriously. "Here try some of this," he offers. I take the proffered ball of black and gingerly start to chew on it. Adara twists a curl round her finger and looks questioningly up at her brother until he passes her a bit as well. As I turn the tasteless but very chewy substance around my mouth, I realise he's been giving himself time to think, to work out what to say.

"I may as well tell you the whole story... it looks as if you'll be with us for some time. You may have noticed our mother's eyes?"

"Yes," I reply. "Where I come from many people have blue eyes, but it's mainly people with paler skin colour, like mine. It often goes with lighter coloured hair." At this Adara touches my light brown hair as if she's been longing to do so but hasn't dared ask. I smile at her.

"I suppose my lighter hair, skin colour and green eyes have made me stand out a bit from the rest of you, apart from my clothes." At one time I would have hated to admit this but now, between my friends, it doesn't seem to matter. "I've noticed your mother is the only one in the Living to have blue eyes. The rest of you all have brown eyes."

"Well, it's not difficult to see. Our mother's blue eyes are what captured the interest of our father. He met her at a Gathering years ago. When a man falls for a woman he comes to live in her Living. He's told us he felt so honoured when she agreed to be his partner. He could hardly believe it. There were great celebrations because father is an excellent hunter and he brought a lot of food and skins to our group. Sometime later, my mother discovered another woman had secretly been hoping to capture his heart. This woman ended up feeling very bitter towards my mother. Eventually, she found another partner but was never happy. He wasn't a good hunter and couldn't supply her with many skins. That woman became Froni's mother."

"Which one of the Living is she?" I ask.

"Well, that's the problem," Rhodri continues, chewing the gum. "Once she'd given birth to Froni, her mother decided she wanted to go with the hunters. She said it was to get more skins. If women want to, they can, but it isn't very often. I wonder now, if it was her way of trying to get closer to our father, without our mother being around. Maybe she thought she could win him through her prowess at hunting. Who knows? Whatever happened, I don't think she was as good as she made out because she ended up getting herself killed by a wild boar who'd been speared."

"Oh, how dreadful!"

"Well, after that Froni's father went back to his own Living, leaving Froni here to be raised by her mother's kin. So Froni, who'd been embittered against our mother in the womb, resents our family. As she sees it, we have both parents, she has none; our mother took away the man her mother wanted and now Froni has no parents left. Everyone in the Living loves her and cares for her but I don't suppose it's the same as having your mother there."

"Why is she nasty to me? She doesn't look nastily at you and Adara, only me. I'm not part of your family."

"Oh, but you are in a way. You've been taken in by us, you look different, like our mother does and she's jealous, I s'pose. She daren't be seen to be nasty towards us; the Living doesn't accept people being unkind to each other. It's one of our rules. Maybe she thinks she can get away with it with you. Who knows what goes on in her head? I certainly don't."

"I've noticed she gives me 'the look' when no one else can see her," I reply slowly. "You know, I've always felt it was my fault when people don't like me. Now I can see it might not be me, but something I represent, which I can't do anything about. I'll try to be nicer to her."

It doesn't make any difference. No matter how pleasant I try to be, Froni continues to glare at me. In the end, I give up and ignore her, not realising it could be a bad move.

One day, Adara comes to me with a glow of excitement. "The bursts of sun are back!" she exclaims. "Shall we go gathering?" Mystified, I follow her bouncing curls. "Here, you'll need this," grins her brother. He hands me a short hazel stick, sharpened to a point at one end that he's been working on for days. Feeling touched to be given the stick, I set off after his sister. When I mention it to Adara, she laughs. "Oh, he's given it to you so you have to do the work, not him!"

The mood spoilt, I can feel a frown forming, as I follow her to a small clearing. In the sunshine, a carpet of green, heart-shaped leaves covers the ground, with the odd star-shaped, brilliant yellow dotted among them. Forgetting my annoyance with her brother, I catch my breath at the beautiful sight. "I've never seen so many celandines in one place before! Don't they look lovely when they're all together."

"What did you call them?" asks Adara.

"Celandines, my mother taught me the names of lots of plants when we went for walks in the woods together. They never looked quite as alive as these though," l finish wistfully.

As we chat, a few more people from the Living appear. I observe them touching the leaves gently and saying something before rooting up a plant, using a sharpened stick similar to the one Rhodri had given me.

"Come on," says my companion, "I'll show you how to do it." Adara explains how we have to thank the Spirit of the Celandine and ask permission before uprooting it, explaining it would be put to good use and appreciated. In return, we must send love to the Spirit of the plant for more plants to grow.

As I follow my friend's example, I think how much better it is to respect plants in this way, rather than tear them up with no regard, as future people do. Soon we've collected a whole bunch of plants, the little tubers gathered below the leaves like bunches of elongated tiny potatoes.

On arriving back at the Living, we hold the tubers by the leaves. Adara reminds me not to lick my fingers, "The raw plants can make us poorly so we have to wipe our hands on moss after touching them."

"What do we do with them now?" I ask.

“Wait and see,” Adara grins.

Gradually more and more people arrive back in the Living with different leaves and more tubers. The fire is glowing in the central pit. We join the gatherers placing the roots of their plants into the embers before carefully wiping their hands on the mossy rocks. As the sun’s brightness begins to wane, Rhodri makes his way in with handfuls of lime leaves, which he adds to the pile of leaves gathered in the centre.

“Now we shall have a feast!” declares Adara. She shows me how to extract the hot tubers from the ashes and blows on them to cool them a little. Next she wraps some leaves around them, slightly cooking the leaves in the process. I’ve forgotten how good it is to eat hot food. Since my arrival I’ve only eaten fresh nuts, berries and leaves and it feels really comforting. Feeling mellow, I smile at Rhodri, handing his stick back, all forgiven from earlier. As I do so, I catch a glimpse of Froni’s expression. The girl quickly masks her look but a shiver runs through me at her undisguised hatred. No one else seems to notice, so I turn my head away and laugh, trying to show Froni I don’t care, as Rhodri pulls a frustrated face about the mud on his stick.

CHAPTER 6
Treeshifting

One day we are sitting together when I suddenly have a thought. "Rhodri, do you remember the first day I arrived?"

"Of course I do," he responds with his cheeky grin. "How could I forget?"

"Well, what did you mean when you said you thought I was your sister and she should do better than that?"

"Oh! He never thinks I do anything very well," retorts Adara, her face flushing.

"I thought she was treeshifting," Rhodri explains rubbing his neck. "It's when we stand with a tree and blend into it, becoming one with the tree. It's a useful skill to hide if we need to. All the children learn how to do it and we play games hiding from each other. I thought you were Adara doing it; until I saw you properly."

"How do you treeshift? Will you teach me?"

"You seemed to be doing a very good job of it, how else do you think you got here?" Rhodri responds.

I'm not convinced about this so the brother and sister agree to show me how to do it. I watch as Adara stands right up against the tree, leaning into the bark, folding her body against the curve of the trunk. The expression on her face changes, she relaxes more and more until it appears that her body and limbs are becoming the same colour and shape as the tree's appearance. A sudden twig

snaps behind me making me turn, then when I look back Adara has completely disappeared. All I can see is the tree.
"Well Rhodri, she did pretty well, I don't think you could complain about Adara this time," I comment. A bird call above draws my attention and when I glance back at the tree again, Adara's back. "Wow! That was amazing Adara!" The younger girl blushes and looks very pleased. "How do you do it?"

Rolling her hair round her finger, Adara pauses while she thinks. "You've got to feel the Spirit in the tree as if they're your friend. Speak to them with your mind. Feel love for them as you would anyone else. Ask them to help you. Everyone sees the next bit differently; I feel as if the tree is hugging me, instead of me hugging the tree. Rhodri, what do you feel?"
"I see my arms as tree limbs, I feel my legs and body become the trunk and my head soars to the top of the tree. Up there I can sense the sap flowing up and down, the branches and twigs become my lungs and I breathe in and out through the leaves. Every leaf glows in the sunlight, pulsing and creating food with the rhythm of my breath. It is a wonderful feeling," he adds with a grin.
"Have a go and see what happens," his sister urges.

I stand very quietly, breathing in and out slowly, while thinking of the tree I'm leaning into. Unlike my future life, I don't have to worry that someone will walk along the path any minute and think I'm a 'nutter' hugging a tree. I can fully concentrate. I start to feel the love I always feel when I'm next to a tree and imagine the tree as a person. I manage a little but not very much. Trying as hard as I can, I know in my bones it's not working. Eventually, I open my eyes and look at my friends. "I didn't do very well," I mutter.

Adara shoots a cheeky glance at her brother, "You did a lot better than Rhodri when he first tried! Don't be put off."

Suddenly a thought passes across the young girl's features, "Do people in the future do treeshifting?"

"No way!" I reply, "Most people would think I'd lost my mind if they thought I'd been trying to do something like this."

Adara looks very sad. "Why do they think that? It strengthens your mind. Losing your mind is when people have terrible things happen, their mind shuts down to cope with it and they can't do every day things."

I sigh. "I am so sorry. The future's not so good. People forget how to care for each other like you do. They don't work together for the good of everyone, they work and work for this stuff called money."

"What's munny?" asks Rhodri. He often seems a bit surprised by what I say.

"It's a piece of metal," then I realise they won't know what that is. "It's something taken from the earth, changed and shaped; many, many are made and people do work, get given the money, then go and buy food with it."

"Why don't they gather the food for themselves?

Then they would know it was good food and they would like it."

"Most people don't know how to do that anymore. They do jobs like building houses, making clothes, teaching children, healing the sick, looking after the bits of metal or helping people to exchange the metal for food."

"Does everyone get the same number of pieces of metal?"

"Well, actually they get money, which is also made of paper. It is worth more." I frown trying to think of how to explain it. "Paper is made from trees. They cut the trees down, chop them all into tiny pieces, press it together and make flat pieces of thin stuff, put writing on it and say it is worth lots of the metal pieces." As I'm explaining this I become conscious of the looks on my friends' faces. They're absolutely horrified.

"Do you mean trees are killed to make this stuff called munny?"

I've never really thought about this before. Having just spent a long time trying to merge with a tree, I realise how callous I must appear to my friends. A sudden breeze whips through the area, making all the leaves shudder, as if the trees are feeling it too. It goes very quiet between us. No one speaks for a long while. Inside I'm burning up with embarrassment and feel terrible, wondering what my friends now think of me. Rhodri and Adara look as if they are in shock.

Suddenly, Adara speaks quietly and thoughtfully, "You have much mind undoing to do before you can learn what we know."

"And you don't know half of it," I think to myself. I decide to be very careful what I say about the future. I must only explain what is absolutely necessary.

I begin to see that changing my ways of thinking and beliefs, is the only way I'm going to fit into this world. For the first time in my life, I realise that never having had the same mind set as other people is actually an advantage.

I think back to Zari and Mina with a smile. They would have screamed in horror landing here! Mina, who's always trying to copy her older sister, couldn't cope without electrical gadgets, nail varnish, make up, clothes and all the adults in her life telling her what a princess she is all the time. And Zari! Zari couldn't manage when they had gone on a school hike and she had to have a 'wild wee'. She'd put on a right performance, until the teacher told her it would make her poorly if she didn't empty her bladder behind the big rock on the hillside. She'd sulked all the way home. No, they really couldn't have done this. I start to feel slightly better about myself. It isn't always about how you look or what you know; sometimes it's all about how strong you are in different circumstances.

I smile tentatively at my friends as we wander back to the Living, and wonder if I'm forgiven for my earlier comments. Rhodri's reassuring grin and Adara's hand squeeze tells me everything I need to know.

Despite my growing happiness, there's a nagging at the back of my mind. I'm still the outsider, as

Froni never misses an opportunity to point out. "Why is your skin such a pale colour?" she quietly hisses when I walk passed her. "You look out of balance."

Another day Froni sidles up to me when no one is looking and spits out. "You look dull compared with all of us, why don't you glow in the same way?" Instead of snapping back as I used to, I decide to try and ignore the words. Despite my efforts, they touch my old fears, deep inside, of not fitting in. I think of the future where at least I belong more than I do here.

With these thoughts playing on my mind, I begin to think about returning home. "Maybe if I can learn to treeshift, I'll be able to go back the way I came?" Although, I often find reasons to criticise my mum, I still love and miss her. I decide to start practicing in secret. Remembering what Adara said, I find a space of my own, sit very quietly, close my eyes and try to think of all the horrid things that happen to trees in the future. Then I try to send lots and lots of love to those trees; with apologies for what my race is doing to them. This is the best I can think of, I don't quite know what else to do.

While I'm sitting concentrating; I suddenly feel a presence nearby. Opening my eyes, the kindly Elder who healed me has appeared. By now I've realised that the Elders come and go as they please. Sometimes they are with the group in the Living space and at other times they disappear for several days. No-one questions them, it's accepted that they are wise and whatever they're doing, it's

right and good for everyone. I remember that this Elder is called Druantia.
"Do not feel bad for your race Jenni; it is not your fault they are like that. It doesn't help the situation; only adds to it. You are doing well sending love. Love is a very powerful force; the most powerful in the universe."
I look up into the kind eyes, so full of wisdom. "Can you help me?" I ask, "I really want to treeshift but I don't know how to undo the way I think. The world I come from is so different."

CHAPTER 7
Elder Wisdom

A gentle smile crosses the ancient face. "I thought you would never ask," she responds. "We cannot teach until we are requested. The student will not learn until they are ready. When they are ready, they enquire."

How different from our culture where we have to learn phonics and counting as soon as we enter nursery. I remember being so envious of friends who'd moved to Sweden. The youngest girl was three; I kept hearing how she had gone to Kindergarten, where the children played all day. I'd been so jealous. She hadn't had to do sit down learning until she was seven. Maybe Zari and Mina would have been kinder if they'd had more time to play. I wondered how different my life would have been. I thought back to the younger me, when I'd been on my own with Mum most of the time, going for walks in nature but not really playing with other children.

I jump slightly as Druantia's voice brings me back to the present. "I understand this is very hard for you. You were not born to this way of doing, yet you are eager to learn, which is what matters. The first thing you need to do is calm the chattering in your head."

And so begins the first of many lessons with my wise mentor. Druantia sits, patiently explaining how to breathe in and out, watching my breath as

I do so. “If a thought pops into your head, don’t think about it, let it go. When you think about it you give it power and it stays and grows. Don’t feel upset with yourself or cross that you are thinking, look at the thought, love it and let it go.”

Gradually, during several sessions, I begin to get the hang of it. Finally, I manage to sit, quietly watching my breath come in and out for many breaths. As I do so, calmness sweeps through me and I begin to hear every sound and rustle around me. “You are doing really well,” my teacher praises. “Now I want you to start feeling the love, which is all around you as you breathe. When you think of love in your mind, how do you see it?”

I don’t have to think about that; I always see shapes and colours when I have strong feelings. “I see a beautiful green all around me. It keeps me safe and sends out rays of shining green light.”

“Now, I want you to go and stand by the tree, there. Do your breathing until you feel really calm and ready. Then allow yourself to feel the green light shining from you. When it happens, ask the tree if you can join together, with your green rays linking in with hers.”

Not entirely sure what I’m doing, I follow Druantia’s instructions. Standing by the tree, I start to breathe. Slowly and surely, the calm comes, then I can see the green love radiating from me. Focussing on one of my rays, I ask the Tree Spirit to join with me. I am totally unprepared for what happens next. My green rays are suddenly engulfed in a mass of other, very powerful verdant rays, swirling and dancing around me. The two sets of rays begin to intertwine, creating amazing patterns of light. I'm swept up in the most divine sensations of pure joy and happiness. It's exhilarating while at the same time very peaceful; but after a while it feels too beautiful to bear. I have to stop it; the intensity is becoming overwhelming. From what seems like miles away Druantia's soft voice enters my consciousness. "Jenni, open your eyes when you need to break the connection, but remember to thank the Tree Spirit first. I am also talking with her, she knows you. She understands. Come back gently, when you are ready. "

Slowly, I open my eyes. Everything around me seems faded after the intense vibrancy of my connection with the tree. I feel exhausted and sink to the ground.

"Rub your arms and hands, wriggle your toes," Druantia advises. "How are you feeling?"

"I don't know," I whisper. "I need some space to think."

"Don't worry. You did really well. You managed to treeshift for quite a few breaths before I could feel your need to return. You are very special and I know now why you were the one to visit us. You have a natural talent; but you need to take time to adjust. Sit awhile, I will return soon."

I sit in a sort of daze, trying to process what has just happened. In a very short while Druantia returns with a sort of bowl, shaped from a very large leaf. Inside is water. She cups the bowl to my lips while the cool liquid soothes my mouth and throat. As it courses through my body, I begin to

feel a bit more myself. The ground beneath me feels reassuringly solid. At last, I feel I can speak, "I never realised it would be like that. It was a beautiful experience but so incredibly powerful."
"The tree has realised that now; she is your training tree. You need to work with the same tree until you are totally comfortable, then you can try with other trees. For now, I think you have had enough. When you are ready to have another go, I will help you."

On returning to the Living Space, I don't really want to talk about my experience to Rhodri or Adara. It feels too personal and too special. I have to give myself time, to let it become a part of me, before other people can share in it. If I speak too soon about it, the magic and wonder will go. Recognising something special has happened, my friends respect my need for silence and let me be.

Snuggling down in my bed of leaves, I drift off into a beautiful dream. In the dream I'm on a cloud, high up. I see an older woman wearing a long green flowing dress. Her figure is slim, the dress clinging to her shape, making her appear very tall and sylphlike. The woman takes my hand and leads me into a large glass domed building; which seems to go on forever. Misty clouds swirl around us as we glide through the space. In the middle, under the dome, the woman sits crossed legged and beckons me to join her. As I sit, I hear a voice telling me that I'm in the Place of Learning. I have to sit quietly and the knowledge I need will come. It's a wonderful feeling; my mind is floating yet energised at the same time. Without realising,

I drift off into another dream where I'm cradled in a green hammock with light filtering down and across me.

Suddenly I wake up. Sunlight is filtering through the leaves above. I gaze up. The dream was very vivid and it takes me a while to adjust.

Deciding to leave the treeshifting practice for a while, I spend the next day or two improving my skills at communicating with the animals and trees to collect my food. I need time to make sense of everything. Adara and her mother patiently continue to teach me, demonstrating again and again how to send out love to the animals and give gratitude for their help. Every time a little creature approaches, sharing its precious food stocks, or biting stalks for leaves to fall into my lap, a shivery thrill always runs through me. One day an injured squirrel turns up and Adienna takes her healing herbs to cure the little being, while its companions sit around watching with their wide eyes.

Finally, I feel ready to try again. I mention to Adara what Druantia said about training me.

"The Elders don't always seem to be in the Living Space. How will I get in touch with her to say I'm ready to learn again?"

"Oh, don't worry," Adara responds smiling at me, "If she said she'd help you, you don't have to find her. Go and sit by your tree and she will appear."

Summoning up my courage, I go and sit in the clearing by my training tree. Aware that the Elders appear and disappear, apparently at random, gives me a feeling of awe towards Druantia. How does she do it? How does she know when she's needed? As I sit, a voice breaks into my thoughts.

"I see you are ready again, little one. We will continue with your training."

This time it isn't so intense, or maybe I know what to expect, so it isn't such a surprise. Either way, I begin to enjoy the experience and manage a little longer. After that my training happens daily. As my confidence grows, Druantia gradually withdraws more and more, until suddenly I realise I'm doing it on my own and managing to treeshift for many breaths.

"Can I show Adara and Rhodri now?" I ask.

"Why are you asking me? If you are ready you will do it."

CHAPTER 8
An Unexpected Gift

Finding my friends, I tell them I've something to show them. As we arrive at my special tree, Rhodri's face breaks into a grin when he realises why we're here. Adara smiles nervously. Watching eagerly, they see me stand by a tree and gradually lean into it. A bird chirps loudly above them drawing their attention and when they look back I've gone. Carefully checking the tree, they see no sign of me, then after several walks round, they hear a laugh. It's me and I'm back.

"You were great Jenni! You've really learned fast," says Adara admiringly. She actually looks proud of me. I feel a shiver of excitement. No-one has ever looked proud of me before.

"I've had a good teacher."

"The best," Rhodri replies with a slight tone of envy in his voice. "Druantia must think you're very special, it's normally our mothers who teach us."

"She has no mother here, silly," retorts Adara.

Being reminded of my mum, gives me a pang of homesickness. I've mastered the treeshifting but it hasn't brought me any closer to knowing how to return. I decide to consult Druantia about it. The trouble is Druantia seems to have disappeared and is nowhere to be found. Several days later, I'm sitting by my training tree, hoping against hope that Druantia will appear. "She said she would come when I need her so why isn't she here?"

I lean back against the trunk, sensing the bark starting to soften as I move. The bond between us is such a good feeling. All I have to do is lean in and the tree sends out her green tendrils of love, enveloping me in warmth and contentment. I respond sending green waves from my heart and we play around, enjoying each other's company. Suddenly I remember my dream. "Were you the green lady?" I ask the tree being.

"Of course," the loving thought sweeps through me, "can you remember where we went?"

"To the Place of Learning," I respond.

"That's right. If you have a question we can go there again."

"How? Last time we arrived there in my sleep."

"Dreams aren't the only way to get there. Blend with me and we can travel there together."

Putting all my trust in her, I allow myself to be enveloped by the swirling green love. Suddenly instead of patterns of light, I see my tree friend as a person, the beautiful green person of her dream.

"Come take my hand," she smiles.

The minute our hands are linked, I find myself back in the large domed room, which has misty edges and no proper definition round the walls. Sitting under the vast dome with my tree companion, I look up expectantly. "What do I do now?"

"Ask what you want to know."

"How do I get back home to the future?"

From deep within the dome, I feel a beam of light pouring down into the crown at the top of my head.

Suddenly it all becomes clear how I managed to travel back in time, and how to reverse the process. With the realisation I can now return, a feeling of loss sweeps through me. I've been so happy in my new life; I can't bear to think of never seeing my friends again. "Can I return from the future?" The light floods my mind again. I realise it's not an easy process. It's very risky and unlikely that I would arrive back in this exact time and place.

Thanking the light, I hold my hand out to the tree lady and we dance down a rainbow of green shades, sliding down the last part until I feel my feet back on the earth and my back against the tree.

"Hello," said Druantia, as I open my eyes, "I see you've been to the Place of Learning."

Confounded I look at her, speechless. How does Druantia know everything?

"You are wondering how I know; as Elders we see much, know a lot but only share our knowledge when it is needed or requested. What did you decide about your visit here?"

"I was told I might never be able to get back. I miss my mum but I love everyone here as well. You have taught me so many wonderful things; I can't bear to leave you all yet…I think I'll stay a bit longer."

"A wise decision," the Elder smiles a sudden flash of brightness. "The longer you are here, the more time we have to perfect your return journey to the future."

"Druantia, can I ask you something?"

"Of course."

"In the Place of Learning the light gave me an understanding of how the tree works to bring me back in time, but it was more of a feeling, not something I can put into words. Can you explain it for me so I can have it in language as well?"

"Trees are the lungs of our Mother the Earth. They are a part of her body. They were here a long time before humans and will be here a long time after we have gone. Every tiny cell that forms a part of the tree holds ancient memories of long ago," Druantia pauses. "Time is like a drop of water in a pond. An event happens and ripples spread out in circles; forwards, backwards and all around it."

I frown, trying to recall something. I remember a teacher once telling us about the Australian Aborigines and how they thought of time in this way. When I was younger, it seemed quite simple. Now however, I've been told so many times that time goes in a straight line, the past is behind and the future ahead; I find it hard to see time in any other way. "Okay, I find it hard to get, but please carry on."

"Well, the trees hold all the waves from these time ripples in their cells. So, when you stood against your tree in the future, somehow, the tree memories helped you to treeshift and brought you back in time - as you understand it - to us."

"But how did the tree memories do that?"

"The cells in the tree merged with your cells and transferred information into your body about our Time. For some reason, your cells resonated with the information, maybe they recognised it from deep in your own cell memories and once they all tuned in together... whoosh ... you were here."

I feel puzzled. "I sort of get it but it is really hard to grasp."

"What do you have in the future that makes a sound?"

"A guitar," I answer. "It's a musical instrument with strings, which vibrate at different speeds and make different sounds."

"Perfect. Imagine you are a little insect. You are sitting on one of the strings. It is vibrating at a certain speed. It is all you know and you think that is how the world is. You walk to the end of the string and find a point where all the strings join together."

"It's called the bridge."

"Fine. You arrive at the bridge and suddenly see there are many strings leading from the bridge. One of them is vibrating at a speed you really like, so you walk up that string instead. When you are on that string, the world appears very different from the first string. Both strings remain there, both are vibrating and playing sounds and both are coming from the same source, only they give you a different view on life. Are you with me?"

"I think so. Are you saying the tree is like the bridge on the guitar? I was on a future string, the tree holds all the strings and as I entered the tree space I felt the Past string where we are now and went along it?"

"Yes, that is it."

"So, that's why it is important to treeshift when I

want to return. When I am merging with my tree I can try to find my future tree string. Oh, thank you Druantia!" a sudden urge to hug the Elder overwhelms me and I feel a rush of love and warmth in return.
"Enough of this, it is time to eat and rest," with these words Druantia fades away and I return to my friends in the Living Space.

As I get back, Cara comes up to me with a big smile. Rhodri and Adara are standing nearby with expectant grins on their faces. I look at them all wondering what this is all about. "Why are you are looking at me?"
"Guess what?" Adara can hardly contain herself. "Cara has been working really hard to create something for you, come and see!" She drags me across to Cara's space in the Living. There on the floor is a tunic like everyone else wears. The leaves are stitched on in a diagonal pattern in a multitude of shades of green.
"To match your green eyes," beams their Auntie. I gasp. No one had ever made anything so beautiful for me.
"Now, you really are one of us," says Rhodri with a degree of warmth I never thought I'd hear from him.
"How does that boy always manage to get to the core of my feelings?" I think to myself, as I beam at Cara.
Slipping into the tunic, it's such a relief to shed my tight jeans and T-shirt, which have started to smell. The new clothing feels loose and airy around

my body, giving me freedom of movement. I grin round at the admiring group who have gathered. "Thank you, thank you so much," I say to Cara, "you have no idea what this really means to me." The responding smile is enough.

Adara is keen to explain all about the tunic and how her Auntie has managed to make it. "The underneath part is made from deerskin," she proudly tells me. "Cara had some left from the last time the hunters were here and she decided she wanted to make you an outfit."
"Do you always use deerskin for clothing?" I ask, my curiosity about this world sparked again.
"Well, deerskin is the softest, but the hunters also hunt wild boar, elk and aurochs. They all have tougher skin and of course the boar is covered in thick bristles, which we press into small pieces of bark to make our hair brushes." Adara picks up one of the brushes and shows it to me.
"So, that's what it's made from! I was wondering what those bristles were."
"Here, have a go," Adara volunteers. I pull the brush through my tangled mass of hair, leaving several of the strands caught in the bristles. The lovely feeling of my hair afterwards makes up for it. "You can share mine until the hunters return with more bristles," the little girl offers generously.
"Oh, you look a lot better," comments her brother, as he wanders up. I can feel my face flush. I turn away in embarrassment, although during the next few days I take advantage of Adara's offer and use the hairbrush whenever I can.

PART TWO
Unconditional Love

CHAPTER 9

The Song of the Earth

A shower of leaves lands on my lap. Squirrels chatter above me as others run up to me bearing their precious nuts. Awash with love for the little beings and the beautiful forest, I sigh. It seems hard to believe that a short while ago I had no knowledge of all this; looking round at my friends I feel so lucky to be here.

"What is the future like?" Rhodri questions. He seems full of curiosity about my life in another Time. The little bits of information I've mentioned must sound so alien to him.

"It is certainly not as good as living here," I reply, "I really don't know where to begin. We have lots of things. We can travel in metal boxes and go wherever we want but it does make the air dirty."

"You mentioned metal before. The stuff you called money was made from it. What exactly is metal?" asks Adara.

"It's stuff which gets dug out of the ground, is heated by a fire until it goes soft or runny, then shaped and changed. It can be made into lots of different things."

"Doesn't our Mother the Earth complain when stuff is taken from her?"

"That's not the only thing which is taken from her," I answer, "rocks are blasted out of her hills to build houses. They blow up the hill with something called dynamite, which cracks the rocks into small enough pieces to be moved. The rocks are carried in the metal boxes using oil; a liquid made from trees which rotted millions of years ago and is found deep under the ground or under the sea. Finally, they use this rock to build houses where we live away from the sun and the rain."

Adara puts her hands to her face in horror. "In the future they destroy our Mother to make a Living Space? Why can't they live among the forest like we do?"

"They would think this was going backwards. People in the future think they are so advanced and clever. There is no forest left here. Most of the trees have been chopped down."

"I think they're stupid!" exclaims Adara with an intensity that I've seen in her before. "Can't they understand that the Earth is our home and our protector? Don't they love the Earth? How can they do this to her? What about the trees? How can they kill their friends like this? Why do humans become so awful?"

Too late I remember the promise I'd made to myself to keep quiet about the future. Now my friends are looking at me as if I'm a monster.

"Why do you let them do this?" Rhodri accuses. "Can't you stop them, tell them it's wrong?"

How do you tell someone, existing thousands of years ago, in a small community of people, that the Earth will be populated with billions of humans who wouldn't listen to one small girl? I can't even imagine what a billion looks like. I gaze round for inspiration. "You see the leaves on the tree above us? Well, imagine every leaf is a person; that would probably be about the same number as all the people living in one of our cities in the future."

"What is a city?"

"A place where there is no forest or woods, only lots of people living in the buildings made from stone."

"Do you mean that so many people live with no trees or forest around them? Where do they get their food?"

It feels like I'm getting deeper and deeper into a maze of trouble. A 'fuzzy cloud of grey' appears round my head. I try to explain about farming and markets and bringing food from other places in the world. The more I describe the future of their race, the more openly upset Adara becomes while Rhodri's mouth changes into a grim line, his face puzzled and angry.

"I don't get it," he bursts out, "why would anyone want to live like that?"

Instantly, the air shimmers nearby and Druantia appears.

"I felt your pain," she says to the children. "Rhodri, Adara you don't need to know about this. It's not important for your life. Come to me, my children."

Druantia places her hands on their heads. As soon as she touches them, they close their eyes; a tranquil look steals across their faces and they lie down on the mossy ground. A flurry of sound makes me turn my head. Adienna is hurrying towards us, her beautiful eyes full of concern.

"Are my little ones okay?" she questions Druantia. "I felt their emotion and upset."

"They're fine now," the Elder replies. "Jenni was

trying to explain what the future will be like, but they are not ready to hear about it yet."

I feel dreadful. Too late I'd realised the effect my words would have. I want to find a hole and bury myself in it. I start to slink away. A wave of love sweeps through me.

"Don't feel bad," says Adienna. "We don't need more hurting feelings flying around! You didn't know. We understand it's very hard for you. The children won't remember what you said when they wake up. Please don't tell them anything when they ask."

Sensing the warmth, I begin to feel a little better. Suddenly feeling much older, I decide to be very careful and side-track any future questions from my friends.

For the next few days I concentrate on enjoying life in the forest. One morning when I wake up, there's a change in the air.

"It's going to rain today!" Rhodri announces. All around me the excitement begins to build. The sense of anticipation is electric as people discuss their favourite places for rain days.

"I love being near the river and watching the water bounce on the surface," one person says.

"I like standing under the lime tree. Its leaves guide the water to wash us and it feels so delicious!" another person answers.

"Where do you like to go?" I ask Adara.

"I love standing in an open space in the forest where I can feel the raindrops as they pound down from the clouds," she answers grinning at the thought. "It is such a special time to feel connected to the sky."

"Can I join you?"
"Of course!"

The two of us and Rhodri stroll off together to one of the open spaces in the forest. The trees part to reveal a sky, which has clouded over and is gradually darkening.

"Look, the rain is coming, I can't wait for the feeling of rain on me and the wonderful freshness afterwards," says Adara. She strips off her tunic and hangs it on a nearby tree. Rhodri follows suit.

I am so embarrassed. I can feel my face going bright red. I don't know what to do or where to look. They obviously think nothing of being naked in the rain. If I don't do the same they'll think I'm really odd. I take a deep breath, pretend this isn't happening and take my tunic off, hanging it on a nearby tree. Trying not to be self-conscious, I focus on the sky above.

Soon the first drops begin to fall. Although I've experienced rain many times in the future, it's nothing like this. Normally as the first drops touch me, I'd be scurrying for shelter. In this warmer climate, the first few drops are like heaven. I feel them touch my skin and trickle down my face so softly and gently, like a fairy finger. As the rain increases, I start to feel a pounding of drops all over my body, as if I'm being massaged with a high power shower. Adara and Rhodri are laughing and jumping around as the precious drops of rain hit them all over their bodies too, rinsing away dirt and sweat, cleansing every pore.

"Isn't this great!" yells Rhodri.

Forgetting my embarrassment, I can't help but

agree. I decide never to moan about rain ever again. The sparkling droplets seem almost electrically charged, as they bounce on and around us. With the water running over me, I feel all my troubles rinsing away. Toned up and sparkling, I'm ready for anything. Gradually, the clouds finish releasing their precious cargo and the sky begins to clear. Rivulets of water are running down our faces as we shake ourselves; rainbows of droplets flying around us.

"How good was that!" says Rhodri, voicing all our feelings.

Why have I never experienced water in the same way before? Why have I always taken it for granted? I realise that since arriving here, I've not had a proper wash. At home Mum nags me every day to wash. It annoys me, so I only ever do the minimum; but now when I haven't been able to soak in a bath or shower for days, I realise how lovely it feels. Funny, how I only begin to value something when I don't have it. I'm beginning to realise how this way of life is helping me to appreciate everything on the Earth. I think sadly of the future where everyone takes so much for granted - wanting more and more - instead of being satisfied with what they have.

We collect our garments from the trees and I feel a bit of relief, as I cover up my freshly clean body once more. As we wander back together to the Living Space, people keep emerging out of the forest looking happy and refreshed. The air has that special, clean smell after rain, when every scent is magnified and you feel more aware of what

is around you. "At least that doesn't change," I think.
People chat quietly, basking in the warmth of the sun, after the coolness of the shower.

Suddenly, someone starts to sing. The sound seems to come from deep within her, as if she's almost letting the Earth use her voice to make a sound. Gradually other people join in. There is no tune I can identify; only tones blending with other tones. Beside me, Rhodri and Adara have closed their eyes and are making sounds too. Sitting in the middle of it all, it seems as if waves of sound are washing over and through me, just like the rain washed away all the stickiness and tightness on my skin. Almost without realising, I discover my voice has joined in with everyone else.

Initially, I am very quiet, not wanting to be noticed, but when no one seems bothered, I begin to allow my voice to get stronger. I listen for gaps in the melody and fill them with a sound, sometimes undulating, sometimes smooth, which matches the voices of the other people. My own voice ceases to be important; what matters is the whole. Everyone else seems to feel the same way, as the music begins to swell and drop, reach a high note, then spiral down, tumbling through harmonies which are varied yet beautiful. Finally, the singers all seem to silently agree that it is finished. The sounds gradually disappear until all the humans sit, in a quiet group, contemplating the feelings of calm and thankfulness of being alive in this wonderful place.

The next day, I ask the others what all the

singing was about. “Oh, it’s our way of thanking the Earth and the sky for the gift of rain,” Rhodri explains, probably wondering again about his guest and how little I know. “We all appreciate it so we sing our thanks. Don’t you ever sing to the rain in the future?”

“Not really, I suppose the nearest we have in the future is songs which someone else has written and we all sing them together.” I reply. Wanting to divert them from more enquiries about the future, I ask, “Don’t your songs have words?”

“No,” answers Adara, a little frown creasing her forehead. “Mother Earth can’t understand the words but she can hear the melody and vibrations in our songs; we are each giving our own thanks, like the birds. It has a lot of power when it comes straight from you. What’s the point of singing someone else’s song? It’s not true.”

My mind goes to all the pop stars in the future, singing their songs with all their fans joining in. No wonder they seem to find it intoxicating. All those hundreds of people singing your song, it would feel very powerful. How amazing would it be if all those people sang their own songs, but harmonised as a whole. I give a deep sigh, it’s all very well thinking about it in this Time but it would be quite another trying to suggest it in the future.

CHAPTER 10
Attack

A few days later, I have a nasty encounter with Froni. Sitting not very far from the river, I'm on my own, trying to practice sending love to the trees. The bubbling and churning of the water in the background soothes me but also masks the sound of the girl's approach.

I don't realise quite how much resentment Froni has built against me since my arrival. Startled out of my concentration, I'm shocked to see her dark eyes narrowing in her thin face, as she approaches me. "Not ignoring me now, then," she sneers, "like you have been." When I don't reply it seems to give her courage to carry on. "You think you're so clever, don't you? I've heard everyone talking about you. You act like a baby who knows nothing of our life, yet you think people like Druantia will teach you. Well one day I'll show everyone, you wait and see. You've no idea what I'll be able to do."

I don't know how to respond. I look at Froni wondering if she is a little mad. Her eyes are harsh and very bright. I feel a shiver of fear but don't want to show it. How do I deal with this?

"Oh, stuck for words are we? Not normally quiet are you, when you're with precious Adara and Rhodri? Maybe it's because I know so much more than you. You think you know it all but you don't. You don't know anything."

As she talks, I see 'spikes of red' shooting out of Froni's head. Fascinated, I gaze at them with my mouth open. I've seen my own feelings in my head before but never actually seen someone else's. Suddenly Froni stoops down and grabs a ball of moss. Then she comes up to me and before I know what's happening, she's stuffed it in my mouth.

"That's what we do round here when someone can't close their mouth. We stuff it closed for them," she laughs unpleasantly, "with the moss we wipe our bottoms with."

I can hardly breathe. I spit it out, bits still caught around my teeth. Froni turns on me again.

"Oh no, you don't!" she yells and pushes more moss into my mouth. Small bits of moss catch in the back of my throat and I start to choke. Pushing away from her, I stumble, attempting to get free. Even at school, no one has ever attacked me like this. I can't believe this is happening to me. Shock ripples through my body. I have to get away. She's mad.

Froni's mocking laughter echoes in my head. Panic swells and tightens my throat. Fear of what else could be in the moss causes me to gag. 'Black and white arrows' fly around my mind, muddling my thoughts; I can't see straight. Coughing and spitting, I stumble towards the river. Without thinking, I head straight into the clear sparkling water. As the cool silky waters flows over me, I relax into the welcoming body, feeling a release from the panic. I swim to the other side, anxious to get away from my tormentor. Only as I emerge onto the opposite bank do I suddenly realise what I've done.

A gasp of horror reverberates above me. Froni is standing on the opposite bank looking at me with a mixture of shock and revulsion. Then slowly her features change. With a triumphant realisation, she calls across to me on the opposite bank. The words are indistinct. I can't hear clearly what she says because of the sound of the river. In my muddled state, all I see is Froni looking triumphant, shouting something. She grins nastily, drawing her finger across her neck in a threatening gesture. Then, taking her time to fully relish my predicament, she slowly turns. Full of the news of how I've broken one of the sacred rules; I can see her heading back to the Living.

The meaning seems obvious. I'm going to die for my actions. I remember the strength Adienna used to prevent me from entering the water. I shiver, realising I won't stand a chance against these fit and healthy women if they decide to capture and punish me. All my newfound happiness disappears in a breath. Shaking, I force myself to think quickly about escape. Remembering how sensitive Druantia and Adienna are to feelings, I know I need to stay calm, so I can hide from them. Breathing deeply, as the Elder showed me, I start to move away from the river; trying to put as much distance as possible between myself and the Living I've betrayed.

Judging that the sun is beyond the mid-point of the day, I decide to keep it behind me and to travel east. I don't know what's going happen but it seems if I'm to keep alive I now have to avoid other humans. That's all I can think of. I have to keep moving.

As I walk, a great sense of sadness engulfs me. I begin to realise what I am losing. My mind turns to Adara and Rhodri, my first true friends. What will they think of me? Cara and Adienna, who've been so kind to me, how will they see me now I've broken their sacred rule? It seems really difficult to imagine them harming me but I remind myself that I am living in very different times. They used to have human sacrifices in the distant past. I remember reading it in a book at school. Does it apply to these days? These friends of mine come from millennium before I was born. How can I understand how their minds or customs work?

Saddened to think my newfound friendships could be more treacherous than my nasty schoolmates, I start doubting myself. Why does everything I touch end up badly? 'Waves of grey' sweep around me, swirling and engulfing me in sadness; suddenly I shake myself. Terror of what might happen hits me like a force of wind. I need to control these feelings otherwise I will be found. Taking deep breaths again, I focus on walking in the right direction, keeping the sun behind me.

As more distance separates me from the Living, I begin to relax a little. Maybe it won't be too bad; I've learnt how to live from the forest. At least I won't starve.

A howl suddenly splits the air, tearing me from complacency. I freeze. I recognise that sound. It's the sound of a wolf. Wolves hunt in packs. All the childhood fairy stories of the big bad wolf flood into my brain. The eerie call comes again. Where is it coming from? How close is it?

My heart seems to speed up. Thoughts race through my mind. How are wolves treated in this world? Are they friendly or not? How would they react to finding a defenceless girl? I'm not prepared to wait and find out.

As fast and as silently as I can, I start to run. I have to create a space between me and the animals. Legs pounding the earth, I try to look where I'm going but it's not easy. Sharp twigs catch on my toes, pain shoots up my legs and soon my feet are bleeding but I daren't stop. Sweat pours off me. The constant thudding of one foot in front of the other takes over everything. I can't think. My breath starts to come in ragged gasps. Branches scratch my cheeks. Fear comes in 'black swirling clouds' surrounding me, blocking my vision and infiltrating my senses. I force myself on and on and on.

Finally, feeling my heart is about to burst, I have to stop. By now I don't care what happens to me.

Gulping in the air with my head pounding and my heart throbbing, I know my body can take no more. As I lean, panting against a tree, my ears scan the forest for any sounds. Small animals rustle in the undergrowth, birds sing in the trees, wind blows through the branches…no howls. Have I evaded the pack? Not wanting to linger, I regain my breath and cautiously start on my way again.

I'm becoming aware that this is very different from a stroll in my local woods. Here there are all sorts of creatures running wild. It's one thing seeing these lovely looking creatures in the safety of a zoo or Safari Park. It's quite another thing being face to face with no barriers between us. Reality suddenly hits home. I'm totally unprotected and very, very vulnerable. What am I going to do? When night falls, I'll have to hide somewhere, but where? Where will I be safe?

Trying to slow my breathing and calm myself, I move on as quietly as I can. For the first time since entering this Time, I feel very alone. The dark fear of isolation gradually creeps in, until I am engulfed by 'grey waves' of sadness. Clouds started to gather overhead, the dull skies powering my darkening mood.

As I walk, another new problem emerges. I am thirsty. When I was in the Living, I walked down to the river and drank from the water pools whenever I needed a drink. Now, I've left behind the only river I know. I can survive by eating leaves and berries, but I will need water.

What should I do? If I carry on, I might not find more water for ages, it may be too late. Also, I don't know who else is out there. What if I meet other people who aren't as friendly as Druantia's Living? I daren't retrace my steps; I have no idea where the wolf pack is. Even if I do find my way back, what would happen if anyone from the Living finds me? The niggling doubts about my friends resurface as my fears take control. Did I read somewhere that they used to sacrifice people in stone circles? Have the stone circles even been built? Does Stonehenge exist yet?

I drag my mind back to my lessons at school. What did I learn about ancient history? Neolithic; I always thought it sounded ancient but I remember that 'neo' means new. So Neolithic must be the latest age. Mesolithic means middle, so the earliest was Palaeolithic. I wish I could remember when they all were. I vaguely recall that in Britain, farming was introduced in the Neolithic times, which started around 6,000 years ago. So far there's been no indication of any farms, so it could be before then. I try to remember when Stonehenge was built. I've always been fascinated by it, but dates were never really very important to me.

I know the last Ice Age was ten thousand years ago. It had stuck in my mind because Mum had mentioned that ice ages happen every ten thousand years and we were due another one. It had excited me at the time, thinking there'd be lots of snow and I could go to school on my sledge. I, also, liked the idea of woolly mammoths roaming around. It obviously isn't icy, so maybe I'm in the Mesolithic Time. Thinking about it I'm sure my teacher said something about the Neolithic builders of Stonehenge. So maybe, the stone circles aren't built yet. But does it mean humans do or don't sacrifice each other? I'm not prepared to risk it. I decide to trudge on.

My throat is dry and I'm beginning to get a headache. With a mouth that feels like sandpaper, I try not to think of water. The more I try the worse it gets. Soon all I can focus on is thinking of how much I need a drink. My mind runs through possible ways to make my mouth water. Suddenly I remember Mum telling me of a man who had been stranded in the desert and sucked on a stone. Not fancying a stone, which had been covered in earth, I realise that a leaf would make a good substitute. I decide to chew one and see if it helps. Looking round I see a hawthorn tree nearby. Apologising to the tree and thanking it, I pluck some leaves.

Feeling a little relief, I stand still for a while, relishing the moisture as I chew. Then I catch the faint sound of water falling. Is it my imagination? No, it's definitely there. I start towards the noise, feeling a glimmer of hope.

Cautiously approaching through the trees, the sound of water becomes louder. Drawn like a magnet, I finally break through the undergrowth and found myself beside a beautiful, tumbling, sparkling waterfall. The rays of the setting sun glint on its droplets, firing them into gold. I start forward, then stop as I remember; I don't want to fall into the same trap as before. Standing at the side of this tantalisingly close lifesaver, I look around for any stone water catchers, like there had been at the Living. With joy, I can see several nearby. Diving across to them, I gulp the water, sucking the sweet liquid down my dry and raw throat.

I'm so intent on drinking that I don't see the eyes watching me. Unaware of the hands reaching out, I suddenly find myself in the strong grip of two powerful arms.

CHAPTER 11
Capture

With a sinking feeling, I realise how stupid I've been. Unlike my welcome in Druantia's Living I'm dragged along behind my captor, and hauled in front of a collection of people sitting around a fire. They all stop eating and chatting and stare at me.

Trembling from head to foot, I try not to show how scared I am. I force myself to look at them. With a shock, I see most of them are men. In the Living it was mainly women, with only boy children and a couple of older men. Then the smell hits me; meat cooking on the fire. In the Living I didn't eat any meat, only leaves, roots, berries and nuts. As I stand there, I'm very conscious of their stares, which are a mixture of curiosity and wariness.

Suddenly I feel very tired, very hungry and quite wobbly. Not trusting my legs to hold me up, I sink down. I'm past caring what happens to me. It feels like I've been through so much, all I want to do is close my eyes and pretend it's a bad dream. A tear starts to trickle down my cheek so I stare at the floor, hoping it won't be noticed. A wave of longing for home sweeps through me, I think of my lovely mum and my cosy bed. My mind goes to all I'm missing from the future; a house to sleep in, enough water to drink whenever I want and meals prepared for me.

I look up with eyes full of tears. Blurred shapes

shift around the glow from the fire. Unexpectedly, I feel a piece of warm flesh pressed into my hands. Blinking back the tears, I look down and see I've been handed a piece of meat from the fire pit. Tentatively lifting it to my mouth, I begin to nibble pieces off. It tastes so good. I hadn't realised how hungry I was. I brush my eyes and try to concentrate on getting control of myself as I eat.

After a while, a surreptitious glance round tells me that no-one is looking at me anymore. Feeling a bit more at ease, I start to look around. I'm in a clearing in the forest. This one has been deliberately cleared, I can see where branches have been chopped and the wood has been used for the fire. The feeling isn't quite the same as Druantia's Living. There's a harder feel in the air, probably accentuated by the carcass roasting on the fire in front of me. The people look very physical, with sinewy arms and muscled strong legs. They have sharp eyes, alert to everything. No wonder I was found so easily. So far, no one's tried to talk or communicate with me, other than to hand me food. I stay alert; wondering what their next move will be.

After everyone has finished eating, the only two women in the group beckon me to follow them. I'm unsure what to do but don't have much choice. We move to a space in the clearing. They lie down on either side of me and gesture for me to do the same, indicating I should sleep. At least I'll get a chance to rest, I think to myself. Surprisingly soon, I am oblivious to everything.

I hardly seem to have shut my eyes when the

dawn chorus deafens me. As I wake, memories of the previous day flood back. Looking around, I notice the other people are waking, but there's always one or two keeping an eye on me. Looking at their strong muscles, I know, with a sinking feeling that there will be no chance of running away. I resign myself to staying for now, until I can work out how to escape.

Conversation isn't as frequent and flowing as in Druantia's Living; it's as if everyone works as one, understanding each other's moves, with no need to talk about what they do. However when they do speak, it sounds like gobbledegook. For the first time I question how I understood everyone and spoke so easily with them in Druantia's Living. Thinking about it, it's very odd that I've been able to communicate with them at all. Going back in time thousands of years ago, the language should be totally different. Even going back a few hundred years it would be hard to understand the language. So, why could I talk so easily with Druantia's group and yet not understand these people? Maybe each Living has its own language? The only person I know who could probably make sense of this is Druantia and with a wave of sadness, I realise I will never see the beautiful Elder again.

As I look around, I can see that my captors are hunters. Near the trees are a set of beautiful precision spears, their flint heads fiercely sharp and glinting when the sun's rays catch them. On the other side of the glade, a member of the group is working on a piece of flint, chipping with such care and delicacy, as the fragile but strong material is slowly shaped. Fascinated, I wander over to have a look. I remember seeing loads of these flint arrow and spearheads in a glass case in our local library, but I never dreamed I'd actually see them being made. The labels often referred to the tools as basic. They wouldn't say that if they could see this man working.

It's as if every fibre of his being is focussed on the task. He seems oblivious to anyone around him. All that exists is the flint he's working on, the stone tool he's using and his hands. Tiny shards of the sharp stone fly off, as delicately, yet with amazing speed, he works his way around the edges, fine chipping them until the sharp blade emerges. Looking at him, I see 'strong orange and purple rays of light' surrounding the head of the craftsman as he focusses onto the flint. This is the second time I've seen colours and shapes around someone else. A little surprised, I look up. As I do so, one of the tall and graceful women in the group gives me a piercing stare. I'd love to know what she's thinking.

I decide it's probably a good idea not to look at anyone for too long and move off to have a wash near the stream. As in Druantia's Living, the water is respected. No one touches the sparkling water of the small river; washing and drinking is all done from the holes in the tops of rocks where the water collects. Dirty water drips onto the ground to be cleansed by nature's own filter system. Even though I appear to be alone by the stream, all the time I can feel unseen eyes observing my every move.

CHAPTER 12
Moving On

On returning to the group, I gaze around again. A tall man with dark eyes catches my look and seems to nod his head at me, before turning away to get on with checking his flintheads. Several adults are cleaning a hide, scraping off the drying flesh into a cup made from a piece of wood, which has been hollowed out. Other people are adjusting the draped leaves around the hanging carcass. Whatever the action, it's all performed with a respect and love for the animal who has died to feed them.

I wonder if this is what made the meat so delicious. I know I was very hungry but was it also the care with which it had been prepared? No wonder we are always getting sick in the future, all the processed food we eat has no care in it. It's probably created and packaged by a machine, certainly nothing like the love and attention that Mum used to put into the food before she was too busy working. Thinking of Mum is almost too much to bear, so I try to focus on my new situation.

In a group, everyone is needed to share the tasks, so it isn't long before I'm being shown, in hand signals, how to collect wood to feed the precious fire. A gentle glow emanates from the fire pit, the embers from the previous night still retaining their heat. One of the men, who has an injured hand, is gently fanning the life back into it, while the tall man with dark eyes indicates I should gather wood from fallen branches and twigs. Moving around the clearing, I manage to find quite a few pieces but it's not long before I realise I will have to venture further away to find more. Trying to look as inconspicuous as possible, I quietly move into the trees, my senses on full alert. As I gather the wood, I begin to relax. As long as I look as if I'm helping them, their suspicions might drop. I finally feel a glimmer of hope.

Maybe, I could do this every day, start to build their trust and they might relax their vigilance. Then I could slip away. But where would I go? My earlier adventures showed me how much I need other humans. It's not easy to survive alone. Then it strikes me. Of course! I'll find a tree and treeshift to get home to the future. It's very risky, particularly without Druantia around, but I lost any chance of being with my friends when I desecrated their water. No, it's now a matter of survival. If I return to Druantia's Living, I'll be sacrificed. Remembering Rhodri's tales, I worry what will happen if I stay with this group. I'll probably get killed or badly injured in a hunt because I'm so inexperienced. I think of Froni's mother and shudder. I've got no choice. I have to return home.

I decide to wait for the right time. During the next few days I continue to be helpful, collecting wood and attempting to scrape the hides. It's not easy and I make a bit of a mess of it to start with, but gradually the patient demonstrations from the others help me to improve. The tall quiet man in particular, seems keen to show me what to do and how to fit in. Before long, I begin to see the wariness begin to subside in their eyes. The man keeps an eye on me more than the others do, but he seems to relax his vigil more as the days go on. Several days later my chance comes.

Collecting some wood, I find I've wandered further away than normal. Glancing up, I see that no one is in sight and there's no sound of anyone nearby moving through the trees. With my heart beating, I move across to a tree who feels safe. The familiar rustling of leaves greet me as I approach, making me glance over my shoulder in trepidation. Feeling my heart pounding, I edge towards the trunk. Slotting into the safety of the bark, it feels like I'm home at last. I start to close my eyes and feel a part of the tree.

Nothing happens. My eyes shoot open. I'm still here. I shut them again and try again. This can't be happening. I need to go home, longing for my mum floods through me. Desperation makes me feel hot all over. I squeeze my eyes shut. Please, please let me treeshift back to the future. Nothing happens. I can't understand it. Where are all the usual swirling greens and the sense of the Tree Spirit? I managed it relatively easily with Druantia nearby; does the Elder need to be there to make it work? If so, I'm in real trouble. There's no hope for me. I try once more, but again nothing happens.

Feeling totally defeated I make my way back into the camp. The others look up at my slow entry; questions in their faces. I try to smile back at them, even though my heart feels like breaking. The realisation that I might never get home is terrible. I want to crawl away, curl up in a corner and bawl my eyes out. It is the one thing I can't do. Even though these people are very kind, I have no privacy to let my feelings go. At home, in the future, I can retreat to my room, yell, scream, shout at the walls and do what I like. Mum will come and check that I'm okay, but she leavse me to it, knowing I need the space. Here nowhere is shut off, everyone and everything is linked. This makes it even worse; I feel trapped.

The following day, I notice that the group are collecting things up and preparing to move on. The skins have been treated, the meat dried in strips and all the rest of the animal, such as hooves and tail, sinew and bone have been parcelled up. Each member of the group is preparing to carry a small pack of food, skins and other parts. I wondered about the other objects. What will they be used for? I'm beginning to realise that absolutely nothing is wasted in this world.

Trying to forget my troubles, I get involved with the packing and soon I'm following the others through the forest, carrying my own pack. I notice the shadows of the trees are falling to the right at the beginning of the day, then as the day wears on, the shadows move to the left. From that I work out we must be moving south. At least we aren't heading to Druantia's Living; that was in the west.

By nightfall we reach a clearing, which has obviously been made before. Smaller plants tangle in the gap between the trees, but it isn't long before these have been cleared and used to create a sleeping space. The man with the injured hand comes forward with the precious fire bundle, which he has been carrying with great care and reverence. I've worked out his name is Ninian. He lights a small fire in the old fire pit and the other people in the group place twigs and wood, which they've collected, onto the blaze. Gazing at the flames helps to give me a little comfort. I decide I'm going to have to go along with the group until I can work out what went wrong with my treeshift attempt.

Absent-mindedly, I chew on the dry meat stick, passed to me by the tall, dark eyed man. I recall how delicious the first taste of meat was in this world. I'd been so hungry and although I hadn't realised it, I'd been craving the meat. In the future, Mum and I are vegetarians. In Druantia's Living, we hadn't had meat, only nuts, roots, berries and leaves. When I'd arrived at this camp and been given the meat, I'd gobbled it down. It wasn't only because I was hungry; my body felt like it needed the red meat. Now though, I'm beginning to crave more berries and leaves again. I'll have to find some tomorrow, I decide.

The next few days follow the same pattern. Rising, collecting up our packs and walking. I wonder where we're heading. As my communication with them is still very basic, I can't work out how to ask. I'm merely aware of walking all day in a monotonous repetition of the day before and the day before that. My legs and feet are increasingly painful but I've no means of complaining. It starts to feel as if I've never done anything else. Tiredness and discomfort combine to make me feel more and more miserable. When nightfall comes I flop on the ground to sleep, only to rise in the morning for the whole thing to start again. Each stopping point is at a pre-cleared place in the forest and I begin to work out that we must be travelling a regular route, going from clearing to clearing.

On some nights, when I can't get to sleep straight away, I watch the people in the group, carving and chipping away with their finely honed flint tools. They shape and create the hooves and bones into needles, rattles and spoons as they sit around the light of the fire, the living flares tumbling and playing over the wood which fuels them. Occasionally they give me a gentle smile as they work.

Many days go by and soon I begin to lose count. I try to keep a tally, but it doesn't seem relevant any more. I've forgotten why I was tracking the days and so I stop; weariness battles with hopelessness as one day merged into another.

Eventually, I notice that there aren't many dried strips of meat left. The camp being set up looks a bit more permanent than the previous one night stops. A flutter of hope makes me think we might be stopping the daily trek. My feet are so sore and every muscle aches. As I drift off into sleep, I'm aware of voices singing nearby.

CHAPTER 13
The Hunt

The next morning, I can see a change in the usual layout of the camp. Normally, the sleepers radiate out around the fire. Today, they've grouped into four huddles. One is in the west, one in the north, one in the east and one in the south. I watch what they are doing. Each person is engaged in a task of making something.

The group in the east has gathered flower seed heads and are carefully and respectfully removing the bright blue seeds from the dark, dried up head and placing them reverently on a leaf.

The group in the north, including the tall man, are weaving together the longer red hair of the deer that had been killed at the last camp. I can see that there are other sorts of hair being woven in. It must be from previous hunts. I can't be too sure but I wonder if the long bristly strand is from a boar; it looks like the bristles from Adara's hairbrush. I recall Adara mentioning that elk and aurochs are, also, hunted. The shorter hairs in the weaving must be from those animals.

In the west, the group are carving small signs on pieces of bone. I wonder if the bone is from all the different animals.

In the south, the group are blowing into cups made of leaves, holding the cups close to their mouths and offering them up to the south.

Curiosity has got the better of me so I watch,

fascinated, wondering what they're doing. As they're working, each group starts to sing. Each song is separate and totally unique, yet all four songs flow in harmony with each other. The sound is a beautiful change from the monotony of the previous days.

After a time, the singing stops and the groups stand. Their completed tasks are held carefully in their hands. One by one, each group offers their gifts to the fire. As each gift hits the flames their song combines with the smoke, swirling upwards. I watch fascinated as a 'blue, streaming light' soars from the top of each person's head to mingle in the air with the smoke tendrils. The final gift is the seeds, which create a spectacular crackling and sparkling in the flames. As this last offering hits the spiralling smoke, the blue lights and smoke combine above the fire, with shapes starting to form out of the swirling mass. Mystified, I begin to see them turn into four animal heads. I watch, entranced, as they become images of the beasts whose hair and bone were in the offerings; the heads of a deer, an elk, a boar and the large horned head of an auroch float ethereally, yet clearly, above me.

A great sigh of combined satisfaction and prayer goes up. Respect and gratitude can be felt from all the humans towards the impressive shapes above them. As the group gazes up at the blue undulating forms, the head of the boar bows towards them. An answering cry comes from the watching people, an eerie, haunting call, acknowledging the meaning of this. The sound lingers in the air. Time seems to stop. I watch, awestruck.

Slowly, as the smoke begins to disperse, the shapes start to dissipate, swirling away into the forest. Soon all that is left are the glowing embers of the fire. After a while, the people start moving quietly away to start their preparations for the hunt.

Conversations I had with Adara and Rhodri come back to me. I remember them telling me that every living creature has a Guardian Spirit, like the wonderful Tree Spirit I trained with when I was learning to treeshift. Does that mean the shapes I've just seen were the Guardian Spirits of the animals? I wonder if the smoke-created head of the boar was giving permission for a boar to be hunted? Looking round I have my answer. People with grim faces are sharpening their weapons and sinewy muscles flex and stretch, as they start to warm up their bodies in readiness for a difficult chase and attack.

I wonder what I can do to help. I know I'm not skilled enough to take part. I decide to collect leaves and berries to fortify the hunters on their long chase. It seems I've chosen exactly the right thing to do. Smiles greet me when I return with a collection of food and start handing it out to the hunters. The tall man in particular gives me a big grin. With a pang I'm reminded of how much I miss my friends and in particular the way Rhodri used to grin at me. The sweet feeling of acceptance mingles with the bitter pain of missing my friends.

Soon the hunters set off, leaving the fire-keeper

and me to tend the fire. Gesturing that I should make myself useful, Ninian sends me to find more wood. Although this would be an ideal time to try to treeshift again, I can't let the fire-keeper down. He has to stay and watch the fire. He's unable to collect fallen branches with his injured hand and I know if I don't find fuel, the precious fire will go out; the last thing the exhausted hunters need on their return.

Remembering to be aware of where the shadows fall, so I can make my way back again, I venture into the forest. The tall trees cast a green light all around me, as I wander from tree to tree, harvesting the fallen twigs and branches.

Suddenly, I hear a noise, an unfamiliar noise, of heavy feet crunching through the undergrowth and then a short squeal. Turning rapidly, my heart skips a beat, as I see I am face to face with the boar. It's much larger than I thought it would be, with long, bristly hair and a twitching snout. I watch it approach, panic beginning to rise in my throat. The boar sniffs the air and I can see it focussing above my head, where 'the black and white arrows' are starting to point in on me, muddling my thoughts. I freeze. Not knowing anything about wild boar and their habits, I don't know what to do. Thoughts race through my head. Should I try and climb the nearest tree? It would be hard and I might not manage it in time. Should I run? Would it run after me, enjoying the chase? My heart is pounding now. Terrified of doing the wrong thing, I do nothing.

The boar comes closer, sniffing the air around

me. His tusks look very big and club like on either side of his snout. I slowly shrink back, feeling the rough bark of a tree against my back. I have nowhere to run. Please, please let the boar ignore me. The snout continues to waver around and the animal's little beady eyes look in my direction.

With astonishment, I see that the eyes hold intelligence and awareness. I've never thought of a wild boar as having any sense, but looking into the animal's eyes at fairly close quarters, I realise there is more to this creature than I expected. It doesn't seem bothered by me, it snuffles around near my feet, then moves away. Relieved, I let out a long breath that I didn't know I'd been holding.

A subtle movement catches the corner of my eye and I see shadows advancing from the trees. Dark menaces with pointed weapons, focus on the beast I've been observing. As if it senses their presence, the boar lifts its head and sniffs the air again. Its pursuers freeze. It saunters forward snuffling the brown rich earth, hidden below the layers of leaves. The hunters advance, silent and deadly; hardly making a sound. I don't know what to do; I daren't move in case I disturb the people and attract the boar's attention to their presence. I shrink further back into the tree behind me, trying to blend in.

All of a sudden, swift and violent movements erupt from all sides. Spears fly with precision. As they hit their mark, the boar lets out a terrible sound; high-pitched pain and terror screams through my ears. A flurry of bodies speed past me; the wounded and dangerous animal has to be stopped from charging his attackers. One man straddles the boar's back and expertly grabs his snout. With one powerful, swift stroke he slices the animal's throat with a lethally sharp flint. In a second, the agonising scream is silenced and the deed is done.

Simultaneously, I see something starting to manifest in the air. Fascinated, I watch as the blue smoky image of a giant boar appears above the dead animal. A wisp of blue floats up from the still body of the beast, to join the larger ethereal being; a sudden and complete silence envelops the scene.

Time stops as I watch the swirls combine and link into the greater shape. The misty creature looks directly at me and I gaze back transfixed. Our eyes lock for a few seconds or is it a lifetime? Time completely disintegrates. Suddenly a gust of wind blows through the glade, the blue shadowy form disperses and I shake my head, uncertain of what I've witnessed.

The bodies around me materialise into the familiar members of the group I've been travelling with. I've never seen anything killed in front of my eyes before. My legs are shaking and I feel sick. I can't get the sound of squealing out of my ears or the beauty of the blue image out of my mind. My companions have no such feelings, or if they have, they are well under control. With a speed and efficiency that I can hardly believe, the creature is skilfully skinned, with a mass of butchered meat piled up and all its organs wrapped with care in various parcels of leaves. Then I realise why. A distant howl echoes across the landscape. A responding howl echoes a bit closer. The humans all exchange glances...wolves. Hurriedly, we gather up as much meat as we can, wrapping each bundle in sweet smelling leaves to disguise the scent of the meat from the wolves. A bundle, dripping with blood, is thrust into my hands by the dark eyed man, and then we're on the move, rapidly and quietly making our way through the trees to the place where we left Ninian.

CHAPTER 14
Journey's End

I'm wondering if my heart will ever stop this loud thumping; it seems to be constantly on alert today. I try not to think of the intelligent beast I observed sniffing around my feet, now a mere lump of meat in my arms. While wondering at the vision of blue, I try not to feel the fear of being ripped to shreds by a pack of wolves, wanting some easy food. Although thinking about it, we did leave a substantial amount of meat behind. With a flash of inspiration, I understand why. It's a decoy to delay them. By sharing it with other creatures of the forest, they will hopefully leave us alone.

Before I know it, we're back in the Camp Space all around the fire. Soon everyone is busy, processing the meat, hanging up strips to dry in the trees' branches above the smoke of the fire. I grin to myself thinking that smoked bacon must have started like this, as a way to protect meat from the wolves. Meanwhile, alerted by his fellows, Ninian is building up the flames in an attempt to keep the animals away.

Darkness falls and still we continue to work by the light of the gleaming fire, conscious of the threat to our hard won food. Finally, the meat is processed and we can sleep. As I lie in the dark, I go over the day's events. The intelligence of the boar's eyes haunt me, as does his scream. In the Time I come from, meat eaters never see the process through, so I can afford to be squeamish. My mum and I don't eat meat and so I feel even more horrified by the loss of life. However, having lived in this way I can understand the need for it all.

These hunters wouldn't be the strong, healthy people that they are without their diet of animal meat. I think back to Druantia's group who all looked slightly weaker, although they glow with a different sort of light. While I was with them they were vegetarian but I remember Rhodri saying they did eat meat on occasions.

Despite being very tired, I find it hard to sleep, lying under the wavy canopy of dark leaves, with the occasional star revealed by the breeze. Gazing up, I try to make sense of what I witnessed earlier. The spirits of the animals appear to have been consulted before the hunt; it seems the Spirit of the Boar suggested that his animal was the one to hunt that day. Maybe there are too many boars in the area for them to live comfortably. The kill was quick, clean and fast, with as little pain to the beast as possible. The food has been shared with other predators, which meant the other boars are free for a while because the wolves' bellies are also full.

If meat is to be consumed, I suppose this is probably a much better way. My thoughts go to the future where the animals are farmed intensively; reared in confined spaces, with no freedom, given a restricted, controlled diet and filled with drugs to keep them from catching diseases from each other in their artificial environment. No. This way is far more respectful towards the animal and to the humans who eat them. I drift into dreams in which blue boars float around me, butting me with their snouts and piercing me with their beady looks. I find myself floating up, up and away into the Place of Learning. I hear a voice telling me that I'm beginning to understand more and soon I will... Before the voice finishes, I am being pushed awake by my neighbour.

The hunt completed, it soon becomes apparent that we're to set off on the long walk again. I wonder where we're heading. As before, one day turns into another, with the routine of walking, eating and sleeping. The more I do all this exercise, the easier it starts to become. My muscles start to feel more toned, my skin's developing a healthy glow and despite all my worries I'm feeling good in my body. Every night I'm so exhausted I drop asleep quickly with few dreams. During this time there's no chance for me to sneak off and try to treeshift again.

Slowly, I'm beginning to understand snippets of the exchanges between my companions. I pick up that our destination is near and excitement is building. I am very curious as to where we're going. I join in with the grins and anticipatory looks.

Finally, the day dawns when we're nearly there. The hunters get up early and I watch as they mix fine powders with water, creating different coloured pastes on large leaves. Using sticks, they start to paint themselves. Fantastic shapes start to appear all over their bodies, swirls and patterns in

vibrant colours. I'm very impressed
by the transformation. As always, I'm the observer, not asked to take part, not exactly ignored but not included. My old feelings of being left out re-surface and I begin to feel 'a wave of grey' engulfing me. I take myself off and sit with my back to a tree. Although I'm physically healthier than before, I feel more cut off than ever.

Later that day, the others set off with joyful and light steps while I drag behind. Why do I never fit in anywhere? The best place I've ever been in my life was in Druantia's Living and I've completely blown it.

As we walk through the trees, a drumming sound starts to filter into my ears. Soon a bubble of noise and chatter rises above it and in moments we burst through the trees into a large opening, which is next to a beautiful small lake. Around the edges of the lake I can see bright pink nodules of rock. I don't have time to examine them closely because a wave of sounds, colours and movement assault my senses. After being so long with small groups of people; it's quite overwhelming.

My companions move off joyfully into the crowd, meeting and greeting friends, acquaintances and maybe family. Who knows? I don't. I shrink back against the comfortable bark of a nearby tree watching the scene in front of me, feeling even more of an outsider. The thought of retreating into the trees behind me and trying to treeshift crosses my mind, but my earlier attempts make this way of escape useless. With a deepening sense of unease, I decide the best course of action is to watch and learn more about my new situation for now.

No one seems to notice me as I observe the mass of people from the safety of my tree. Soon I begin to identify individuals among the group. There's my hunting companions of the last weeks chatting with other similarly painted hunters with more animation than I'd seen in all the time I was with them. I wonder what they're discussing. Maybe hunting techniques, maybe details of the tracking and killing of the animals. One of the listeners reacts to the stories with excitement and runs off into the crowd.

I let my attention wander to another group; they're looking at each other's clothing, comparing the leaf colours and designs. Looking around I notice a distinction between the groups. Some people are dressed in animal skins, very finely processed and finished, whereas other people are dressed in the leaf garments. I suddenly begin to realise that the clothing I'd taken for granted in Druantia's Living is actually very beautifully crafted. Among the 'leaf clothing people', I start to see distinct differences. Each group has its own finely designed way for the leaves to combine. Some leaf garments cling to the body, so that it almost looks like they are moving trees, very well camouflaged. Others have looser garments, which flow almost like cloaks around them. The leaf colours are different as well. Some people wear the leaf colours of fresh spring, other people wear the darker green of summer, while some are in the vibrant multi-colours of autumn. Then I see that each of the hunter groups seem aligned to one of the 'leaf' groups. With a sudden sense of horror, I realise that my companions of the last weeks are talking to a tall woman, dressed in a familiar leaf style. As she turns, I feel a shudder of recognition. It's Adienna.

My friends' beautiful mother looks across the area, scanning the faces with her piercing blue eyes. With my heart thumping, I shrink closer to the tree and try to sink lower and lower desperate to make myself invisible.

"Well your treeshifting skills haven't improved I see," comes a familiar voice in my ear. Terrified I look up to see Rhodri grinning at me. I turn and run, taking the quickest route away from the crowds, full of fear of what will happen to me.

"Stop," Rhodri yells. The fear and terror of when I'd left the Living, floods back; 'black swirling clouds' surround me, blocking my vision and infiltrating my senses. I have to get away. Despite the hurt look on Rhodri's face, I daren't stay to explain. There's no way I'm ending up as a sacrifice. It's all clear to me now. From what I remember from the history books, strangers were sacrificed at gatherings like these. I've been lured here, captured by pretend kindness like Hansel and Gretel, only to be sacrificed to their Gods. Well they can think again. That's not going to happen. They'll see.

I need to think quickly. What can I do? I'll never outrun the hunters, so I'll have to hide. My heart pounding in my chest, I scan around for somewhere safe to go. Voices seem to be getting nearer, panic mounts in my throat. Suddenly I see a hollow in a tree. Trying to trick my pursuers, I run in a different direction, then double back and dive into the hollow, covering myself with leaves. As quietly as I can, I slow my breathing down and stay as still as possible.

The running comes nearer; I hear shouts and hold my breath. My heart is so loud I'm sure it'll give me away. Blood pulses in my ears as I hold my position, not daring to move a muscle. The footsteps wander around my hiding place, I hear a few mumbled comments and leaves are scuffed in the area. 'Cloudy bubbles and black and white arrows' confuse me, I can't think straight. All I can do is wait.

Finally the sounds start to retreat. Staying as still as I can, I don't move an inch until I'm sure they've gone. No human movement can be heard. The birds start singing again, little scuffling noises of mice and squirrels return and the normal sounds of a forest with no human interference resumes. Feeling safe, I peek out of my hiding place.

Sitting opposite me, with her eyes firmly fixed on me, is Druantia. Looking at the ground, I feel utter defeat. I push the leaves aside and sink my head into my hands. All the tensions of the last weeks give way as a torrent of tears flow uncontrollably down. Druantia sits and waits.

CHAPTER 15
Understanding

After a while, I look up, drained of emotion, expecting to see anger on the Elder's face. Instead I see something very different. Understanding, care, even love suffuses the wise woman's eyes. Then she speaks.

"You have been through a lot little one," she starts. "Why did you leave in such a hurry?"

"Why?" I start, "You know why. Froni must have told you."

"She told me you had run off and you had polluted our river water. She had great delight in conveying that message to me."

So Druantia definitely knows. My heart sinks even lower.

"What is my punishment?" I ask, dreading the answer.

"What do you mean punishment?" answers the Elder.

Shaking with fear but determined not to show it, I whisper, "Froni drew her hand across her throat. I thought it meant I would be sacrificed for harming the river."

The older woman looks long and hard at me. I feel she is looking deep inside and sees everything. She sees the torture I've gone through, the fear I've experienced and the terror of what might happen to me. I am shocked when she gives me a beautiful, loving smile. I'm still not sure that this isn't a trick though. I decide to play along for now, it's all I can do.

"You behaved terribly by entering our water. You understand how important it is to keep the water pure and clear. Polluted water means sickness for us all, so it is essential we keep it clean. After Froni told me about it, I had to send messages to every group downstream from our Living, so no one drank or used the water for four days, to prevent sickness."

This is terrible. She's making me feel so bad. Why doesn't she get on with it? I'm a gonner anyway now. I hang my head in shame, waiting for what is going to come next. "I had to perform a special cleansing ceremony to ensure it was pure enough, apologise to the Water Spirits and re-energise the water crystals so they became healthy again. All this took time, which should have been spent on other matters, like looking for a lost little girl from the future who'd run off and was causing all manner of trauma among her friends." Did I hear that right? Did she mean they were worried about me? I look up in surprise.

"Do you mean me?" I ask in a small voice.

"Well, people from the future don't pop in every day of our lives and I have responsibility for you."

I play for a bit more time. If they care about me, will they still sacrifice me? Maybe I can argue my way out? I have a go. I speak quietly, as that normally works well when I'm in trouble with a grown up. "I know it's no excuse but in the future people go in the water all the time. No one there has the same respect for water. I wasn't thinking, I

was upset at what had been said and done to me, so I escaped. It was only when I'd crossed the water that it hit me what I'd done. I'm really very sorry to have caused so much trouble." Then I take a deep breath, "What will happen to me now?"
Druantia looks long and hard at me. I am acutely aware that my life lies in her hands.
"I think you have learnt your lesson. You have much to learn about our world and the way of things here. What do you think the word sacrifice means?"

Shaking now, I realise I have to speak it out loud. "In the future, people believe that in your times people were sacrificed to appease the Gods, on stone tables and in stone circles. They believe that people were killed in this way."
The Elder looks at me and her mouth drops open. She looks horrified.
"Is that why you ran away? Did you believe we would kill you?" The anger in her voice scares me. "I don't know which is worse. The lack of trust in your friends or the fact that you believe we would do such a dreadful thing to you, our guest. Let me inform you that the word must change its meaning in the future. In our time, sacrifice means giving up something sacred. You polluted the river so all our Living and other people beyond had to give up our sacred life-giving water for four days, using the stored water in pools near the flow. If you had stayed with us, the punishment would have been to see how that affected your own Living and others. As it was, you disappeared, missing out on understanding how much trouble you caused. On

top of that you caused more worry for all the Living wondering what had happened to you."

Intense feelings of relief and shame seem to be fighting it out inside me. I hang my head, not sure of what to say. Druantia looks at me and her expression softens. "I don't know where this idea of killing people to please the Gods comes from," she says. "We all walk and talk to the Spirit of Creation on an equal level. Every day we ask for help and ideas to assist in the way we live our lives. In that way we stay in balance with what is around us, the world continues to be beautiful, feeds us and gives us all we need. What more can we ask for? The future you talk about seems very strange in comparison."

It's all overwhelming. "I've been too much trouble. I wish I had never arrived here. I don't know why I am here. I seem to cause nothing but upset. You'd all be better off without me. I've tried to go home but I can't seem to manage it. I appear to be trapped in the past, causing problems and not being able to do anything about them."

"Stop right there, young woman." Druantia orders. "You are descending into self-pity and helplessness which will get you nowhere. I promise we will help you return to the future and this Gathering might be the place to start. Many people come here to meet. We exchange ideas, talk and share our creations. Old friendships are renewed and new relationships are formed. Old memories are passed on to the next generation so we never forget where we come from and our responsibilities to our land. It is a very special time that we look forward to every year. So, now you need to start enjoying yourself, forget all the past and find your friends who have greatly missed you. This is a time of celebration and joy. We don't need any grumpiness around!"

With that, the Elder fades away, leaving me with as many questions as before, but different ones now. 'A cloud of pink euphoria' floods my senses as relief overwhelms me. I begin to relax for the first time in weeks. It starts to sink in that I don't have to avoid my friends any more and that I can communicate properly again. I still don't get why I can talk with Druantia and all my friends, but couldn't understand the hunters. It doesn't really matter though. What matters is that I find Rhodri and Adara.

Returning to the opening in the trees, I step out into the crowd feeling a little more confident. Scanning the many heads, I search for them. Suddenly I feel a big squeeze. I jump and turn round, as a pair of arms enfold me. Adara's massive hug makes me catch my breath. Laughing, I hug her back. "Oh, you have no idea how wonderful it is to see you again and know everything is all right."

"Why did you disappear?" Adara asks. "And why did you run away when Rhodri found you? He's really upset. He thinks he's done something bad to you."

"It's a long story," I reply. "Let's go and find Rhodri and I'll explain to you both."

CHAPTER 16
The Gathering

Sitting with my friends by a tree on the edge of the Gathering, it feels that I've come home. I've missed my friends' chatter so much. I tell them about my adventures and then sit back, relishing the ability to talk and be understood. I mention how l couldn't understand the hunters and ask if they can explain why.

"Look around you," Rhodri states. "Can you see each hunter group is matched up with a Living?"

As I look, I realise that my earlier ideas were right and Rhodri has confirmed it. I see my hunter companions mingling with Druantia's Living.

"Do you know those hunters?" I ask Rhodri.

"Of course," he laughs, "one of them is my father."

"They can't be. They don't speak like you."

"Yes they do and I think I know my own father," he smiles.

"But I didn't understand them. I don't get this. I can talk to you and everyone in the Living, but when I was travelling in the forest with them, I couldn't understand a word they said."

Rhodri frowns. "Well, I don't know. It's something you will need to talk to Druantia about, she understands many things that we younger ones don't."

"So who gets to go hunting and who stays behind?" is my next question.

"Well, when a boy's voice becomes deep and when

a girl's breasts have grown, then we go through Initiation. It is a special ceremony, which teaches us how to hunt the animals, how to pray to the Animal Spirits and how to understand what the Spirits are telling us. Then, when we are ready we go on our first hunt." Rhodri looks at me enviously. "You got to go on a hunt without any initiation; I wish I'd been there."

I shudder, recalling the look of the boar before it was killed and the sound of its screech. "No you don't. It's not as fun as you think it will be," I snap.

"So, that's why there weren't so many men in the Living when I arrived. They were all on the hunt. In the group I found there were some women as well. Who chooses which women go?"

"The women themselves choose, like Froni's mother did. She was an exception. Normally it's young women don't have a partner yet. If they have small children then they often choose to stay in the Living; I've noticed women changing when they become mothers. It is a very important role and highly valued. We believe motherhood is a great honour. Some women choose to continue hunting, but not often. If they do, others will watch their little ones while they are away. No one is ever left out or uncared for. The well-being of the group matters above all. Remember Froni's mother? There's also the danger of being killed during the hunt. Probably another reason there aren't so many mother hunters."

"Is it also when someone has given life they find it harder to take life?"

"Possibly, I hadn't thought of it like that," he responds.

"Have you two finished chattering?" interrupts Adara. "Listen, the drum is beating for the feast; I can't wait to try all the different foods. We get to eat meat again...I love the smoked boar that our hunters make." I suddenly remember the package I'd been carrying. "I have some in my pack," I explain. "What should I do with it?"

"You need to take it to the collecting place near the fire. Everyone places their food there and we all share it out. We've already put our nuts, berries, hawthorn and lime leaves in the big stone hollows."

I follow as they wander across to the large stone hollows in big rocks near the fire space. I see the familiar slices of smoked strips of meat laid in one of the hollows and place the contents of my pack beside them.

"Mm, I can't wait," says Adara, licking her lips.

"There'll be no treeshifting for you for a while then!" laughs her brother.

"What do you mean?" I ask.

"Everyone knows you can only treeshift when you haven't eaten meat for a while," Rhodri explains. "Meat lowers the speed your body vibrates at, so it is impossible to resonate with the Tree Spirits. You can only communicate with them when you vibrate at their speed."

"Is that why I couldn't treeshift when I was with your father and the other hunters? I'd been eating meat with them?"

"Of course," he replies, "it's obvious."

This boy's attitude really gets to me sometimes. How am I expected to know all these things? He's been brought up surrounded by these beliefs. I've had a completely different upbringing among people who don't believe anything unless science has 'proved' it.

Adara seems to notice my frown, "Come on Jenni, forget it, let's eat." At the mention of eating, I discover I'm really quite hungry. It feels good to taste the leaves I've missed, mixed with the juicy meats. All the hunters have brought different meats, many of them smoked to preserve them on the journey. The leaf-clothed people have brought a variety of leaves and berries from their areas and exclamations of delight can be heard, as people sample flavours which are unlike their usual diet. People grin as their favourite local delicacies are enjoyed by others. Eventually, everyone's bellies are full. As the eating slows down, chatting resumes between old friends and relatives who have moved to different Livings. The drum beat begins again.

Adara claps her hands in excitement. "It's the storyteller," she crows, "I love this part of the Gathering. You don't want to miss him…come on." She drags her brother up by his arm and comes over to me. "You are staying with us," she says, "we don't want to lose you again." Standing between us and linking our arms, Adara marches us across to where the crowds are settling on the mossy ground, in preparation for their favourite entertainment.

I glance around the group, noticing several familiar faces. Friendly smiles and waves greet me until my glance rests on the small face of Froni.

The girl scowls at me and turns her head away. To start with I feel bad, wondering if she'd got into trouble over what she did to me. Then I think of all I've gone through because of that girl and stop feeling sorry for her. I turn my head away and focus on the storyteller.

The drumming is becoming slower now, it seems to be beating in time with my heart. As the drum goes quiet, a soft singing begins. Gradually more and more voices join in. As before in the Living, there's no particular tune, merely people's voices singing and tuning in with each other. Rhodri and Adara's voices join the group and without realising, I start to make sounds with my own voice. Gently at first, I meld with the others; as they rise, I rise; as their sounds go lower, mine match them. After a while I'm totally lost in making the music. I join with everyone in the group in a glorious harmony that soars and falls like a bird swooping and diving in the joy of being alive.

Eventually, the song starts to fade. Dusk is falling, the fire in the centre of the group glows and it's as if the whole group is one. From the centre of this failing sound, the voice of the storyteller emerges. He stands by the fire, arms gesturing, as the sky turns deep velvet and the multitudes of stars in the darkening background slowly grow brighter.

"Deep in the old Time," he begins, his rich voice resonating round the expectant faces, "before the Time of Ice, we lived in very different ways. It was a Time of Giants. People had come from out of the sky and they helped to create a race of beings much larger than ordinary humans. At first, everyone got along. The giants helped the humans and the humans helped the giants. It was a good time to live and humans flourished. Many years passed and they all lived in harmony together. While the giants worked, the people gathered and collected food for everyone. It was a time of plenty, the giants helped to grow large trees, which produced massive fruit, which fed many humans.

During this time, people learnt how to create changes in the environment around them. Crystals were used to make many creations that performed marvellous things. People were very proud of their achievements; they believed no one had ever been so advanced. For a while all went well but after several generations people started to change. They began manipulating the Earth for their own greed, not the good of everyone. Wanting more power, they started to misuse the crystals. The giants saw what was happening and were sad. The giants passed on messages from the people who came from the sky. They warned of what would happen if the people didn't listen to them. A few people paid attention, but not many. The others were so caught up in their power and greed that they had stopped caring for other people or the Earth. The giants knew what would happen so they started to prepare a place of safety for the few people who did care.

These places were built in the middle of the Earth; north of the sea which has no tides. As deep as a mountain, under the surface, a great plate of crystal was created. Knowledge from the Star People helped. Many underground passages and tunnels were created above this massive crystal. They were made so the water and air flowing through them was pure and healing. The giants helped them to move great rocks.

Magnificent stepped pyramids gradually grew above these passages. Nothing as tall or as wonderful had been seen before in Middle Earth. They were created from stone, bound together with a magic substance, which the giants made. This magic substance was like grey water but thicker. When it dried out it became solid and held the hill of stone together. Many ordinary people travelled for several moon passages, walking across the lands to see this wondrous place. Beams of energy rose from the centre of these great pyramids, connecting with the ships, which came more and more frequently from the sky as the building was completed. It was said there was a doorway from these massive stone steps to the stars. The giants helped this to happen. And so it went on.

Meanwhile, the people who were greedy ignored this building. They laughed and mocked it saying, "Who has need of stone buildings as big as hills when they can live in buildings of crystal that shine and emit power that radiates round the Earth?" Using this power they burnt and fought each other, trying to take more and more power. Power is a sickness of the soul."

CHAPTER 17
Wisdom from the Past

The audience sighs collectively. I realise that they've heard this story many times, their reactions punctuating significant points. I wriggle my position into a more comfortable pose and continue to listen, spellbound by the tale.

"One day, the giants collected together all the good hearted people who had walked to the pyramids or helped to build them. They sat on the stone steps. It was an amazing sight. The steps were covered in humans; old and young, mothers, fathers, children, grandmothers and grandfathers all sitting, waiting to hear the wisdom from the stars. The giants explained that a day would be coming soon when they would have to go underground for many generations. They told the people that only humans who could work together and be understanding of each other would survive. Being selfish in those conditions would not work. As they sat there, the giants transmitted memories and ways of being into their minds. They taught them how to grow their food underground and how to harvest the water. People learnt how to sit quietly and find their inner powers and strengths, how to journey in their minds to other stars and how to communicate with the star people. The giants told them that all this had to be done before they could live underground.

Then, everyone was given the big choice: to leave

for the stars or stay behind to create a new race of people. At the end of the changes, which were coming, these people would repopulate their beautiful Earth.

Many hard days of discussion, soul searching and debate was had and families were torn by those who wished to leave and those who wanted to stay. Eventually, the people who wanted to leave accepted their fate, as did the people staying behind. The giants couldn't stay in the times to come. Resources would be too scarce to feed them and the underground tunnels too small. So they left with the sky ships, taking the people who had chosen to leave.

Slowly the conditions outside began to worsen. The weather became colder and colder, then terrible burning rays hit the Earth from the sun, killing any living thing in their path. The selfish greedy humans, who resided elsewhere in their crystal powered buildings, were caught in these blasts of energy. They thought their technology was above the powers of nature but they were wrong. Soon nothing was left of their way of life or culture.

Gradually, the ice advanced. The people inside the great pyramids were warm; the Earth was a constant temperature, the air and water there invigorated them and made them healthier and happier than they had ever been before. Working together, they created the basis of a new way of living. They sat quietly, learnt about themselves and their connections with the stars and prepared for the time when they could emerge from their underground chambers in safety. The beam kept them in touch with their star friends and when the weather was deemed safe they ventured out for short periods into the light and cold of this different world. They didn't stay out there for long though, the comfort and wellbeing of their underground home pulled them back in again.

Finally after many, many generations of dwelling this way, the days started to happen when they felt the warmth returning. Gradually, the people started to emerge and spend more and more time out of the tunnels. They looked around the stone pyramids, which had housed them for so long and saw that great swathes of the steps had been covered in soil and debris from the ice. Small plants were starting to grow again and they realised that one day their underground home would be hidden from view. It would come to look like an ordinary hill covered in trees and grass.

For many years they lived nearby, returning to the tunnels to heal themselves and replenish their energy as they adjusted to the new world and its climate. Finally, the people decided to leave their Mother Pyramid and set off in the four directions to populate the freshly beautiful world. The star people had told them that the climate would be fine now for many generations, as long as they remembered the laws of the planet; how to pray to her, how to keep in balance and how to keep themselves in balance on the inside. When humans' minds are in tune with the Earth, then the Earth will remain in balance."

The storyteller pauses and looks around.

"And that, my friends, is where our ancestors came from. Our story reminds us never to use our Mother Earth for selfish reasons. The people who survived are those who work together for the good of all. We are the survivors who migrated west. Other people went south, east and other people travelled directly north. In this land we have come to the ends of the Earth, beyond this land is a Great Water. Some people have walked to the edge and come back to tell us of its limits. As the Memoriser, I recall this story is the truth. It has been in memory and passed down from generation to generation, to keep the understanding of the past alive, so we can all benefit. I thank you for listening."

Slowly the charm of the voice recedes and people around me start to shift their positions. Caught up in the magic of the tale, I find it hard to move. It takes Rhodri and Adara all their time to get me to their sleeping space.

I lie awake looking at the stars. This is a completely new way of looking at history, very different from the stories I've heard in school. It means that people have been so-called 'civilised' with advanced technology before the Time I come from in the future. I wonder about this. Everyone in the future is always so sure of themselves so convinced that they are the highest on the evolutionary ladder. This story means history doesn't go in a straight line; it goes in cycles.

Logically, this makes total sense. Every natural thing on Earth goes in cycles and circles. Civilisations rise and fall, look at the Romans and the Greeks. The tides rise and fall around the coastline. The moon waxes and wanes every month. In school we studied the life cycles of butterflies and frogs. Everything goes in a circle, apart from man-made things like roads and square buildings. What would happen if we applied nature's way to our homes? I remember Mum showing me some beautiful houses, which were made in circles. "How wonderful to live like that," she said. Maybe some of Mum's ideas aren't so wrong after all...

On the day after the story telling, some of the hunters are working with nodules of the bright pink rock, which I saw near the lake when I first got here.
"What is that rock?" I ask Cara.
Cara is quieter than her sister and since she made my leaf tunic, I've felt a special link with her. Sitting a little distance from the lake, Cara is enjoying the sun's warmth as it twinkles and reflects on the smooth surface of the pure clean water.
"It's the reason the Gathering is here," her soft voice tells me. "As you may have realised, all of our tools are made from flint, so it is incredibly important to us. The pink flint is only found here, by this lake, which is fed by a sacred spring. The water is magical. It never freezes, constantly bubbling with purity. The Elders realised that our beautiful Earth was telling us to notice this site. They asked some wise and generous people to start a Living nearby to protect it. During the short

shadow days we gather here, pour our love into the spring and give thanks to our Mother for this sacred place. One hunter from each Living is allowed to choose a nodule of the pink flint to carve into a special flinthead. Their fellow hunters choose them for their skill and care."

"Oh, who has been chosen this year from our hunters?" I ask.

Cara nods to a young man whom I recognise. He was the eager, fast hunter who grabbed the boar and expertly sliced its throat, so quickly that it hardly had time to realise what was happening.

"Maedoc is the choice this year," she smiles a knowing smile. "It is a great honour in more than one way. There is no better way to capture a young woman's eye than to be carving with the pink flint. It was the year Arthfael won this honour that Adienna became his mate." It's then that I notice the group of hunters are surrounded by admiring young women.

"We may be going on a journey soon," Cara says mysteriously. Annoyingly, she won't give anything else away, despite my best efforts. In the end I give up and wander off to find my younger friends.

Rhodri and Adara run up to me. "We've been looking for you! We want you to meet our father," says Adara, her brown curls bouncing with excitement. "We know you've been travelling with him but you didn't realise who he was." As we walk towards the tall, strong, yet wiry hunter, with the dark eyes and even darker hair, I realise with a shock that he was the man who kept an eye

on me and made sure I'd had enough to eat. It's beginning to make sense now. It feels good being able to thank him for his kindness. In turn, he tells me that he was glad to have kept me safe. Rubbing the heads of his children, he grins, "These two would have never spoken to me again if I hadn't have protected you."
"But how did you know who I was?" I ask.
"Druantia sent a message to look out for you. She knew we were on the other side of the river and that you had headed in our direction." He grins slyly at me. "We don't only use our hunting skills for tracking animals. It wasn't pure chance that we came across you when we did."
"I don't understand how I couldn't understand your talk then, but I can now."
Like his son, Arthfael can't supply the answer. "You'll have to ask Druantia," he responds.

Since our discussion in the forest, I haven't been in a position to talk to the respected Elder. I've seen her talking with the storyteller and in deep discussions with various groups, but never quite near enough for me to speak to. I give a big sigh. I'm beginning to learn that the answers only come in time. I'll have to wait.

CHAPTER 18
Auroch Danger

A few days later, Rhodri runs to find me in great excitement. “The hunters have been doing fire ceremonies and have been promised auroch. There will soon be the chance to hunt and I will be able to watch!” He’s beside himself with anticipation. He hops from foot to foot and can barely keep still. His cheeky grin is wider than I’ve ever seen it. His animation is infectious and I can’t help but smile back. Rhodri points out the open ground on the opposite side of the lake, rich in grass and close to the warm waters. It’s a tempting place for animals to feed, making them an easy target. “Normally, the hunters get here before everyone else and the hunt is finished by the time we all get here. This is quite unusual. I can’t wait!” I can’t share his enthusiasm but I know this is very important for him. He’ll finally witness the skills of his father. Misdirected missiles or charging half-killed beasts won’t be able to reach us and the families of the other hunters. We’ll be safely watching from the other side of the lake. It doesn’t make me feel any better though. The memories of the boar hunt are still too fresh in my mind.

Soon the hunters are banding together and preparing themselves. I feel a sudden wave of anxiety, making me unnerved. I glance at Rhodri. He appears totally unconcerned, gazing at the hunters, drinking in every detail. I shake my head and tell myself not to be silly. Rhodri has grown up with hunting; it's part of his life; not like my future where the most dangerous part of getting food is crossing the road to get to the shops.

A warning call echoes through the soft chatter, quiet sweeps across the crowd. The spectators sit silently on looming rocks or settle into matted grass on the banking. Blending into the background, their natural clothing creates a perfect camouflage. At a quick glance, the people dotted along the banks of the lake are invisible. Alert and ready, the hunters spread out in groups, melting into the trees on the edge of the clearing. Arthfael has secreted himself well, blending into the forest.

Very soon, the sounds of beasts approaching alert us. Heavy hooves vibrate the earth and the rustling grows louder while small bleats of calves intermingle with the deeper rumbles of their mothers. Suddenly the first beast breaks from the cover of the woodland, heading for the richer open pasture. I stifle a gasp. The boar was big enough, but these creatures are enormous. Flouting large and piercingly sharp horns, they wave their gigantic heads from side to side, sniffing the sunlit rich grass. More and more of them stomp into the open area, some bellowing to their mates, some with small calves in tow. As we watch, we can see how the smaller, lighter coloured animals are followed by the calves, whereas the larger, darker creatures are heavier and thick set. They must be the bulls. Their heavy steps make ripples in the earth. The cows in the future are easily half their size. I'm worried for Arthfael and the others. If one of these cattle decides to charge, they won't stand a chance. I try not to imagine the sound of crushing bones.

Acutely aware of the danger, I watch as the hunters work as a team. One group edges slowly to isolate a few beasts, while others position themselves among the trees. Suddenly, a single spear flies through the air, silent, deadly and precise. It's followed by a volley of other spears hitting all the animals in the smaller group. For a moment, the hunters are at great risk. Every watcher holds their breath. Will the remaining beasts charge? It has been known. The cries of the wounded animals alert the rest of the herd.

Sensing danger, the leader, a great hulking bull lowers his horns. My heart is beating so loudly, I'm sure it can be heard. A tense silence links us all. If the bull decides to attack any of the hunters, it will be deadly. The wounded animals groan. The bull seems to be assessing the situation. Suddenly he lifts his horns and races back into the safety of the trees, the thunder of the following hooves shaking the ground. A sigh of relief washes around me as everyone seems to release their breath at once.

In an instant every wounded beast is straddled by a hunter, pulling on the horns and baring their necks. A second person is suddenly by their sides, flint knives already slicing into their necks. Blood gushes forth. It seems the worst of the danger has passed.

A second later, a movement catches my eye. A wounded bull, which has been overlooked, has staggered to its feet. It sways and seems to be gathering its strength. With an awful fascination at how it could move so quickly, I watch it beginning to charge. A cry leaves my lips as it careers towards a man. With a growing sense of terror I see that it is Arthfael. He's just dismounted from the back of a beast that he and his partner have dispatched. Too late he notices it. He spins round and tries to jump out of its way but the animal is in pain and angry. It runs at him, horns down. Arthfael dodges to one side, but the bull turns towards him again. He then starts to run, trying to avoid those lethal horns. My mouth is bone dry. This can't be happening. Time seems to slow down, I feel helpless as I watch the unfolding scene. Willing it not to happen, I watched with nauseating horror as the unthinkable happens. Before anyone can do anything to save him, Arthfael is on the floor, speared by the great beast.

A second man runs at the creature from the side and slices its throat, while another spears it again in its side. Finally it falls with a sickening thud, with Arthfael still attached to it. A shocked silence holds the onlookers. The remaining animals are all dead or dying now, so the other hunters run around to shield the wounded man and see what they can do to help him. A figure detaches itself from the onlookers and races to the other side of the lake. Adienna is by her partner's side in minutes, assessing his wounds and giving quiet orders, asking for moss, herbs and water
from the pure lake. Other healers from different

Livings converge on the scene, bringing the plants they know can help and soon the other hunters have to move away, as the healers work together to try and save the man.

Rhodri and Adara stand frozen to the spot, shaking. I put my arms around them, a feeling of dread sinking into my chest. Why hadn't I listened to my feelings? Why hadn't I said anything? I feel so guilty. I glance at my friends; Rhodri fidgets, fear and anxiety written across his face. I can tell he desperately wants to help but knows he'll be in the way, so he stands thinly, wracked with worry, angry at being so helpless. Adara's fingers habitually twirl her hair, her normally bright face creases into an unfamiliar frown. With blank eyes, she looks towards the bunch of people. Her hair is in a tight knot now around her finger but she hasn't even noticed. I gently coax her to sit down, vainly trying to help. Moments seem like days as we watch and wait.

After what feels like forever, the group around him loosens a little. Some of the hunters weave a platform with their arms under the wounded man. Gently and with great care, they lift him.

"Where are they taking him?" Adara asks in a quivering voice.

Rhodri replies quietly, "I think they will be taking him to the Healing Space. I noticed it when I was looking round after we arrived. It is a shelter made from stone, near the water." His voice sounds hollow and sad.

"Someone told me this place was made to attract the big beasts, but we all know danger is never far behind." He shudders and shakes his head. He mustn't appear weak or he'll never make a hunter. "I never dreamt when I was walking past the place that my father would end up in there. He is normally so careful..." Rhodri's voice tails off.

"What will happen to him?" Adara's strained voice cuts across his thoughts.

"The healers will work on him and then he will need to rest," her brother replies, I can hear his voice trying to sound hopeful. I wonder how confident he really feels. A small voice in my head tells me it could be their father's last place of rest in this life. I violently push the thought from my mind.

The day drags on. Listlessly sitting around is all we can do. I try to encourage them to go for a walk but they don't want to go anywhere. I don't blame them. I've never known my dad but I know what I'd feel like if that was my mum. I brush that thought from my mind. It's too horrible to go there.

The sun is much lower in the sky and the intense warmth of the day has faded when Adienna finally comes to find us. As she approaches, the other two rush up to her, eager to hear her news. I hang back a bit, filled with trepidation, not wanting to intrude. Her blue eyes instantly read all our feelings.

"Don't look so sad," she starts, "it is very likely that your father will pull through. Luckily for him, this happened at the Gathering, where many wise Elders and clever Healers are altogether.

Between everyone he's getting the best treatment possible. The nearby Living has a very talented

Healer who has offered to tend to him until he recovers enough to walk; then a message will be sent to our Living. They think it will take a few moons."

I feel a glow of relief as the other two visibly relax. I look carefully at the woman trying to see if it's merely comfort words, but then feel annoyed with myself. Why would their mother give them false hope? She's such an honest and loving person, but she wouldn't spare them if there's no possibility of his recovery. No, it must mean he has a good chance. Feeling better than I have all day, I squeeze Adara's shoulders in a big hug. The small girl gives me a grateful hug back. Rhodri allows the hint of a grin to flit across his worried face. "Well, that's okay then," he says, relief softening his frown.

Slowly the cloud of worry begins to lift from everyone. After a day or so, we start returning to the normal activities of the Gathering, a bit quieter than usual but trying to get back to everyday life. We go into the forest and gather berries, meet with some children from other Livings and half-heartedly swop stories of where we live and the food we can find near there. They ask me lots of questions but I feel tired of trying to explain where I come from. The excitement has gone and we are ready for the Gathering to end.

PART THREE
Respect For All Of Life

CHAPTER 19
A Slip in Time

Soon the Gathering comes to a close. We are finally allowed to visit Arthfael in the Healing Shelter and find him looking a lot better than expected. He tells us it won't be long before we see him again in the Living. Adara beams and Rhodri allows his cheeky grin to surface. It feels as if a great big cloud has been lifted from us. In turn, the other two explain that we won't be going straight home either. "I've heard," Arthfael responds with a grin. "I hear Maedoc has been finding happiness with a woman." I remember the conversation with Cara and wonder if I'll finally find out what Cara meant by her mysterious words.

As each different group prepares to leave, many hugs are exchanged, with some family members clinging to their last goodbyes until next year's Gathering. Adara explains to me excitedly that Maedoc had found a mate so arrangements have been made to make sure the young lovers are firm in their decision.

"It's good when this happens, all our Living gets to visit another Living and taste their food. This one is by the Big Water, I've never been there before but I've heard there's lots of really different food! I can't wait."

"Isn't it many days walk?" I ask reluctantly, thinking of how far it was to the sea in a car, never mind on foot. My long march with the hunters is still fresh in my memory.

"Of course, but that's all part of the fun. That's why we have the Gathering during the short shadows, so we have time to visit other Livings when the days are long and our energy is high," she retorts.

Soon we all set off. Druantia's Living are walking with the Living of Fedlimid, who's the woman to capture the eye of Maedoc. I finally understand what Cara meant now. Maedoc has been rewarded by his fellow hunters and now gains the bigger prize of having secured himself a mate. Well it's definitely his year. "At least Fedlimid won't have to worry about her meat supply," I think to myself. Some of the younger hunters, who are close to Maedoc, are coming to see their companion settled in his new home. The rest are staying with Arthfael because he will need an escort when he's finally ready to travel. In the meantime, they will hunt and support the Living, in exchange for the healing Arthfael recieves.

The two groups mingle and chat as we walk, making the time pass quicker as the sun rises higher in the sky. I decide this long walk won't be so bad, now I'm with my friends and know what's happening.

Fedlimid's Living is much bigger than Druantia's. I look around at the swollen numbers. I can recognise maybe twenty or thirty people from the familiar Living but they are easily outnumbered by three or four to one. It doesn't seem to matter. Cara's chatting animatedly to another young woman who glances around her a lot. I wonder if she's looking for a mate for herself. Rhodri follows my gaze.

"That's Fedlimid's sister talking to Cara. I reckon she's looking round our Living for a mate now her sister's been successful," Rhodri grins, echoing my thoughts. How does that boy do it? It's as if he reads my mind.

We're following a pathway through the forest, which has been trodden many times by animals and humans. I wonder if in millennia this will become a road. Many roads follow old cart trails, which in turn followed old pathways. It feels strange to think that one day this might have cars racing along it. As I start to lose myself in this thought, it's as if I can hear the cars and smell the petrol fumes.

Rhodri's voice suddenly comes from a long way off, I hear him calling Druantia in a hurried way. I'm not too bothered by him; I'm fascinated by the fact that I can imagine the cars so clearly, it's almost as if I'm actually there. It's so real, I see the tarmac road, the dirt encrusted hedges and I can even see a discarded plastic bag in the ditch. In my daydream I step out into the road. Suddenly a car comes racing by and swerves. A horn blares loudly, brakes squealed and I can smell the burning of rubber.

A pain shoots through my arm, as someone grabs me and pulls really hard. I yell out. Seconds later, I'm back in the forest. My whole body is shivering and I can feel the blood has drained from my face. Druantia is holding on to me, her face suffused with concentration. The others stand round, watching silently.

"How did that happen?" my voice sounds unlike my own.

While the others look at me quietly, I turn and look at Druantia. The Elder is very pale and is visibly shaking. Adienna suddenly takes charge. She tells everyone to set up a space to sleep for the night and then gently leads Druantia away, settling her on a mossy mound under the branches of a spreading oak tree. A sharp voice speaks into my ear.

"You are nothing but trouble. If you've harmed Druantia with your silly behaviour, I'll make your life unbearable." Turning quickly, I see Froni slinking away. I don't need anyone else to tell me to feel bad. I feel terrible. My head droops as I walk away, tears dropping silently.

A little hand slips into mine. Looking down I see the kind face of Adara.

"Don't feel bad," she whispers, "Many mysteries seem to happen around you. It wasn't your fault."

"What did you see?" I quietly ask.

"Well, you were lost in thought and suddenly you started to fade. Rhodri yelled for Druantia. She appeared, like she does, then as she reached out and grabbed your arm, she also started to fade. The next moment, there was a horrible, loud sound and a bitter smell of burning. Within a few breaths you were back and Druantia was looking terrible."

"I need to go to her, it's my fault."

"You can't do anything. Are you a Healer?"

"No."

"Well then. My mother is a talented Healer, she will do her very best. We will all have to rest here until Druantia's strength returns, so the best thing you can do is help me gather some food."

With that, the young girl takes me by the hand and leads me away. Other people from the group are doing the same, subdued and quiet now, where they'd been chatting before. I feel a few eyes on me but when I catch them looking, they hurriedly glance away. I feel really bad. I suppose Adara is right, we have to eat and at least it keeps me doing something.

I can't understand it. What happened? I try and work it out. I'd been thinking about the future and what might be there. Then I drifted off in what I thought was a daydream. But it wasn't. It had become real. I must have actually been there. The car had obviously seen me. How could it happen? I wasn't treeshifting, which was the only way I thought I could slip through time. How did Druantia manage to come and get me? It must have taken massive energy from the Elder. That must be why she looks so pale and drained. With a shiver of fear I realise the car could easily have hit me. How did that work? Why is this all happening to me? Round and round the questions swirl in my mind. I wish I could do something for Druantia. I feel so bad. Every time it comes back to this kindly and gentle Elder. She seems to hold the key to so much, but what is it? A deep sigh escapes as I try to concentrate on collecting food.

Later, as I lie in the space we've all created, trying to get to sleep, Adienna appears. Her dark hair looks tousled and messy, her beautiful eyes are tired with the lack of sleep, yet she's bothered to come over to tell me not to worry. Druantia's going to be fine, all she needs is rest. Then she slips away, back to her patient. I am so grateful to her for coming to tell me. Relief and exhaustion take over and I can finally drift off.

After a couple of days rest, Druantia seems well enough to move on. A group of women surround her as she walks, protecting and supporting her. I daren't approach her, feeling I've done enough harm already. Trying to keep my thoughts in the present, I concentrate on the high sunlight filtering through the leaves, the dappled shade and the myriads of birds singing and chattering in the trees. Occasionally, we hear the sounds of larger animals nearby, at which the hunters prick up their ears and become alert, but none come near enough to threaten or harm the group. As we have enough meat for now, the hunters don't want to waste more time stopping to kill and process the food.

CHAPTER 20
Stranded

Finally, after many days of walking, the smells start to change. A saltier smell drifts in the air and it feels cooler.

Every time I've been to the seaside it's always really special when I first see the sea. This is no different. I may be thousands of years in the past but it still feels the same. However, I'm not in a car like normal. I'm on foot. The seaside isn't full of ice cream vans, fish and chip shops, windbreaks, buckets and spades. As we get nearer, the sun glints on the sea, the beach is covered in sand, rocks and shells, I can hear the sea birds calling but that is all that's familiar.

The shore stretches along the coast, empty of modern concrete buildings. Instead many small dome-like structures are dotted along the higher ground, out of reach of the high tide. They fit in with the windswept landscape, muted colours blending into the background. The sky towers above them, clouds mounded in soft white piles, the sun firing up the blue beyond. Adara and Rhodri gaze open mouthed at this vast expanse. They must rarely see a sky so large, living among the trees all the time. As their gazes rest on the sea, amazement shines out of their eyes. I smile, remembering how it felt the first time I went to the beach.

Nearby is a cone-shaped building covered in

animal skin. As we approach, an Elder and a young child come running out to greet their returning family. Hugs and exchanges of news are passed between them and Druantia steps forward to greet the Elder. Some of the other members of the travelling party wander off to other cone buildings dotted along the shore, doubtless to enjoy a similar welcome home. Fedlimid's family welcome us all into their Meeting and Cooking Space to share a feast of shellfish, which had been cooking on the hearth. The feast has been prepared by the elderly and the very young who were too frail to have made the long journey to the Gathering. Adara and Rhodri have never eaten shellfish and it amuses me to watch their expressions as they try the chewy food. I've never been a great fan but I'm hungry enough to swallow a few and be polite.

Talk goes on long into the night, full of tales of the Gathering and the journey. Concerns about Arthfael are mentioned, with reassurances about the healing abilities of the Healer tending him. Fedlimid proudly introduces Maedoc to his potential new home, while everyone else looks around with interest, noting differences and maybe ways they could improve their own Living. Froni sneakily starts poking her nose into the baskets around the edge of the room and then glares at me when I catch her eye.

Finally, it's time to sleep. The additional group means there are too many to sleep inside and I'm relieved to see that we're sleeping outside under the stars, away from the smoky stuffiness of the building. A fire is lit from the one inside the cone and Ninian sits by it, keeping it alive and watching out for danger. Long days of walking have worn me out and sleep comes easily with the soothing sound of the breakers on the nearby shore.

The next morning we are awake early and go down to the beach. Adara and Rhodri are entranced. They stand watching the waves crashing onto the sand and seem amazed by all the new smells and sounds.

"That sound never goes away," Rhodri marvels. "I was so tired last night but it took me a while to get to sleep with all the splashing of water nearby."

For once I know more than they do, having spent lots of holidays by the sea. We wander along the beach and in the middle of the wide sandy stretch is a rocky outcrop standing alone. A dark enticing cave at the base beckons us in, while above, the weather worn rocks held tempting footholds to encourage climbing. Above the craggy footholds, a tiny grass plateau holds a solitary tree clinging to the peak. I love caves, so I dance across the sand and lead the way, treading in the soft surface, deeper and deeper into the dark cavern shape. Adara hangs back, nervous of what might in there, while Rhodri follows closely behind me.

The sand is banked up towards the back of the cave and that is where I find it. I call out to Adara to see if she's okay, then an echo reverberates around the walls. I love finding places which echo and am excited to share it with the other two. However, Adara doesn't seem impressed. Her eyes grow very wide then she turns and runs, pelting for the entrance. I think Rhodri is just as spooked but he pretends he's concerned for his sister and runs after her. His arm is protectively round his sibling's shoulders, calming her, when I saunter out with a grin on my face.

"It's only an echo," I call, "echo, echo, echo," the walls repeat. "Come and play with it, try making any sounds and see what happens."

It takes a while but I eventually persuade them that the sounds are harmless and coax them back into the cave. We have loads of fun playing with our voices and making daft sounds. Time passes, we play on, blissfully unaware that the tide has turned. Finally, I notice that that the waves are sounding louder and closer than when we first entered the cave. I run down to the entrance and am horrified to see that the beach has been covered in waves, swirling and eddying around the cave's mouth. Running back into the cave I grab my friends' hands and tug at them.

"Come on, we've got to get out!" I yell.

Too late, I see the line of seaweed, marking the tidal reach. Above the line are no rocky shelves that we could climb on to. Knowing the power of water and the relentless thunder of the waves, I realise how dangerous it'll be to get trapped in here. Already the water's grabbing our feet and trying to pull on us as each surging new wave floods in. Splashing outside, I look up.

"Come on," I urge, "it's our only chance!"

I start to climb the rocky outcrop, finding footholds and looking back to check the other two are following. Rhodri's fine but Adara looks terrified, her lip's trembling and her normally happy face is creased with worry. Feeling guilty for putting my friends in danger, I swing back down beyond Rhodri. Just in time, I manage to grab Adara's hand before a large wave pounds in and sweeps the little girl off her feet. Rhodri sees what's happening and comes back to help. He holds on to me as I grip Adara as tightly as I can.

"Don't let go!" I scream above the crashing surf.

The waves suck out again, trying to wrench Adara from my grasp. Using both hands I manage to pull my friend free of the water and drag her, bruised and shaken onto the rocks. Without waiting I push her ahead, desperate to get onto the higher ground. The grass growing on the top proves the sea doesn't normally reach up there. Rhodri helps his sister and minutes later we're on the summit, panting and gasping for breath. Adara stands pale and shaken, clinging to the small tree.

I look around. The wide sandy beach has gone and in its place, an ever increasingly turbulent sea crashes and churns round the foot of our sanctuary. I've always been fascinated by how the transformation of a beach takes place with the incoming tide, but that's normally from the safety of the cliffs or the promenade, not from an isolated rock in the middle of the sea. Turning to the others I apologise.

"Are you okay now Adara? Oh that was so scary back there. I'm so sorry I forgot all about the tide. I'm afraid we're stuck here for several hours till the water goes away again."

Adara looks at me as if I'm mad. Rhodri frowns at my words. I repeat myself, trying to make it clearer, explaining about the tides and how they work. Puzzled by their expressions, I stop speaking. Adara speaks. Then it's my turn to look confused. Rhodri speaks but the same thing happens. I can't understand him either. It's as if I've gone back several weeks to my time with the hunters. My friends are suddenly speaking in a completely different language, which I don't know. I'm hurt. Here we are stranded, all alone for hours to come and they're excluding me from their conversation by speaking in a language I don't understand. Are they punishing me for getting them into this mess? My old fears of being excluded re-surface.

"Okay, you've had your fun now, speak normally to me." Maybe I'm a bit sharper than normal but I'm annoyed. Adara says something and Rhodri answers, they obviously understand each other but they don't look as if they're having a joke. Their faces seem concerned.

I begin to panic. What's happening? Why can't I understand them anymore? Did I bang my head when we were climbing up the rocks? Did I do something with the echoes in the cave to distort my understanding? "No, don't be silly. Think logically," I tell myself. Something is different from normal. What is it? Apart from being stranded in the middle of the sea with the tide steadily rising around me, nothing much...water surrounds me...water everywhere. Every time I do something silly it is connected with water. The first time I swam across a river, which separated me from Druantia's Living; then I couldn't understand the hunters. Yet when we all met up with Druantia again in the Gathering, I could. Now we are trapped, surrounded by water and it's happened again. What is it? Ideas churn in my head like the waters below me.

Meantime Adara and Rhodri are looking more and more terrified. They cling to each other, watching the waters rise.

"Of course," it suddenly hits me, "they have no concept of the tides. They think the water will keep on coming." Feeling more and more frustration at not being able to communicate normally, I wrack my brain as to how to explain without words. I gesture to the water, raise my hands up and then lower them. That doesn't help a lot. They look fearfully at me, as if I'm the one controlling the water. I shake my head. Pulling lots of faces and moving my hands, I try again with more gestures, until eventually they seem to grasp what I'm trying to say.

"The sea will go back," I keep saying, moving my hands towards the horizon. Maybe by repeating it I can get through to them. Their faces soften and a little of the concern seems to fade. They still huddle by the small tree, as if its very presence is a comfort to them.

Exhausted with my efforts, I lie down on the small patch of grass and close my eyes. This seems to reassure the others. We all doze, lulled by the crashing music of the waves. I'm feeling hungry and I'm sure the others are as well but none of us want to risk going down near the waves where the sea harvest can be collected.

CHAPTER 21
A Puzzle Revealed

A while later, when the shadow of the tree is getting longer, I open my eyes and notice the waves aren't so loud. The tide is finally going out. I gaze across the beach and see the sand reappearing in strips.

"It won't be long now," I grin at the others, forgetting they can't understand my words. They seem to pick up on my tone and smile back. Soon, enough sand is exposed for us to pick a path to the main strand. Desperate to reach the security of the shoreline, I lead the way. Not expecting a response, I comment, "Well, I don't want to do that again in a hurry."

"Neither do I," responds Adara.

I turn in surprise. "I understood you again!"

"Same here," she replies.

An immense feeling of relief floods through me, "But I still don't understand..."

"Ask Druantia," replies Rhodri. "That's what we all do when we don't understand something."

It's easy for him to say that but Druantia never seems to be alone so I can ask her.

As we walk back, Adara voices her fears. "I was so scared. You started yelling at us in words we didn't understand, then you made us walk through the water to get out of the cave." Adara shudders at the memory. "Why did the water try to grab me? Was it because we had walked in it? Rhodri and I talked about it when we were on the rock. We were worried that the waters were rising to show us we had dirtied them." Her voice shakes a little and I can see how frightened she has been.

I feel terrible again for putting my friends in a position that endangered not only their lives but went against their beliefs. Desperate to reassure her, I think of the best way to explain it.

"This water is different," I start, "The water wasn't coming to get you, it is something called the tide. Every day the water goes higher and lower, twice a day. As we stay here you will see it happening. I know it is a terrible thing to go in the water of the river, but that is because we can drink it. You can't drink this water. It is very salty. I'm sure that will make things different."

Later that day, my theory is proved right.

As the sea starts to come in again, one of the people in Fedlimid's Living wades into the water accompanied by sounds of shock and horror escaping from the lips of their guests. Glancing at my friends, I see a slight smile on Adara's lips and a definite smirk on Rhodri's face as they watch.

The river dwellers are persuaded to try a tiny bit on their tongues. We giggle at the disgusted faces pulled. Once it's accepted that the water can't be used for drinking, the visitors soon get used to wading cautiously in the water. Very wary of the waves, they only venture in the shallowest parts.

Gradually, as the days pass, their confidence builds and it isn't long before several members of Fedlimid's Living share their fishing skills with the visiting hunters. They stand very, very still on a rock by the sea, hardly moving a muscle. A sudden movement, a flick of the wrist and then a fish is landed on the beach; wriggling and squirming as it fights for its last breath. Maedoc is clearly impressed, he studies and listens carefully, trying to learn the technique.

Food is plentiful along the shore. We go collecting shellfish from the pools and rocks and sometimes we're lucky enough to find crabs. We learn which seaweed to collect and take it back to the cone shelter to be cooked.

One morning I finally manage to be by Druantia's side as we are preparing some shellfish. It is odd, normally there are other people all around but on this morning I'm totally on my own with her. It's an opportunity not to be missed.

"Druantia," I start, "may I ask you something?"

"You may."

"Why can I understand everyone when we are all together, yet when I was alone with the hunters, I couldn't? I've been trying to puzzle it out. Oh, and something else, the other day, when I was cut off on the rocky outcrop with Adara and Rhodri, we didn't understand each other. Was it because I'd been silly and forgotten about watching out for the tide? The other two were new to the seaside but I knew about it. I should have been protecting them but I didn't. I think it has something to do with my behaviour. It seems to happen when I've done something silly. Is it a form of punishment?"

Druantia looks at me, a long hard stare, which goes deep inside, right to my furthest secrets. I begin to feel a little uncomfortable.

"Is that what you really think?" she asks. The old lady looks very sad. "I watch and listen to you and fear for the future and how the world will change. You've talked about this thing called punishment before. Why do you think you are to blame? What are you taught to make you, a child, think you are so bad?"

I falter, then answer quietly, "When something goes wrong, I think I've caused it."

"Oh, dear child," Druantia says, "of course you haven't made it happen. It was me."

I look up in surprise. "You? How?"

"Think about it, every time you lost the ability to communicate, what was separating you from me?"

Suddenly it dawns on me. "Water! Of course! That was the other thing I had thought of, I realised water was involved each time but I thought it was my actions to do with it."

"No, my little one, I maintain your ability to understand the others. I know you come from a very different Time and the language we speak will have changed immeasurably during the millennia to your Time, so I have used a secret of mine to assist. Maybe in time to come you will learn about this secret, but it is not for now. Sadly, I cannot maintain the ability over water, so if you become separated from me by water..."

"As I did when I crossed the river and recently, when we were cut off by the tide?" I interrupt eagerly.

"Exactly so," is the response.

"So, if I want to speak to everyone, it's in my interest not to be separated from you by water?"

"Exactly."

At that moment, my friends appear with a basket of shellfish they have collected. When I glance back, Druantia has done one of her disappearing acts and I know the conversation is ended. Only after she's gone do I remember what else I wanted to ask her. Oh well, I suppose my question about that weird slip in time will have to wait.

Everyone from Druantia's Living are fascinated by these woven baskets. They're made from a bendy reed that grows where the river joins the sea. Lots of tiny rivulets slow the water down and the plants grow in abundance. Adara's eagerly taking lessons from one of the women and has already developed quite a skill at the craft. It's amazing how quickly new skills are learnt when people meet and share ideas.

In my own future, the Internet is the way people and ideas are linked. In the right time and space I can see its value, although I can, also, see how useless it would be in this world where people live completely from the land. I don't like to admit it but I am beginning to see that Mum's arguments do have value. If I'd had no understanding of plants or trees, I'd have struggled much more when I was lost in the forest. My knowledge helped me to know which leaves were safe to eat and how to read the sun for direction. These are things that help you to survive. In the modern world, this isn't so important, but one day it may become important again. My mum obviously thinks it will be. Who knows what might happen?

"Come and help us, Jenni!" Adara calls out.

I settle down to prepare the food for our next meal,

not bought from the supermarket, as in the future, but collected freely from the Earth around us. Mum wouldn't ever have to worry about money here, I reckon she'd love that.

Thinking of Mum produces a wave of homesickness. I decide to ask Druantia about returning to the future as soon as I can. I love my life here, but it isn't my Time and I have a nagging feeling that there is something I have to do in the future. I'm not sure what it is yet, but I won't find out unless I return.

CHAPTER 22
The Message

Time is moving on and soon our time by the sea has been marked by the passing of a full cycle of the moon. Druantia is aware that her Living needs to be back in the forest before the shorter days make travelling back a much harder task. The fascination with their new environment is pulling less on the people and they all start to feel a yearning for their familiar landscape of the forest and bowers of hawthorn.

Cara confides in me that the month with Fedlimid's relatives, has increased Maedoc's desire to be with her. He's fascinated by the woman and the place she lives. Happy to see him content in his choice, his family and childhood friends realise it's time to part. It doesn't stop the tears from flowing or the promises of meeting next year, particularly from Maedoc's mother. I feel sad for his mum but then Cara explains that she will see him again at the Gathering and maybe in time, there will be little ones.

She points out that children are the future and they are treated with love and kindness in every Living. The stories remind everyone that treating children well creates a secure future whereas treating them badly can create many future problems. His mother likes the girl Fedlimid and trusts her to love her son as she loves him. Pride in her son's ability to attract a lovely mate seems to

fight with her sadness at saying goodbye.
I watch as the two Livings prepare to part and realise how important these ties are. This is why the larger Gathering takes place every year. I'm beginning to understand what a major event it is, for everyone.

Soon we're on our way again. As the pattern of daily walking resumes, I remember what happened on the way here and carefully control my thoughts, trying to remain in the present, enjoying the trees, the birdsong and the chatter of my friends.

After another moon cycle of travelling, we seem to be reaching familiar territory. To start with, I was amazed by how the others negotiated the vast forest, which seemed all very similar. However, the longer I spend in it, the more I recognise the differences between one area and another. The sorts of trees and how they grow subtly changes, as does the terrain. In some areas it seems much flatter, whereas in other areas there are definitely more hills to climb. Sometimes, the trees grow like cathedrals towering above us with arched avenues, elsewhere the trees are a little younger, closely packed and dense with hardly any light filtering to the ground below, making the undergrowth bare and the ways easier to navigate. In some parts of the forest trees have fallen with age, their rotting carcasses feeding a myriad of other plants and creatures; while the gap created gives smaller plants the chance to flourish in the unusual pools of sunlight. Occasionally, we come across a marshy area, with lakes puddled between the vast trees, giving rise to another variety of life.

When a river crosses our path, we have to follow the banks until a fallen tree trunk or massive rocks help us to cross the precious water without touching its clear, glistening body. Travelling as part of a larger group, I feel much safer. The nightly howls of wolves can be heard, sometimes quite close, but I know the skilled hunters are always protecting us.

Finally, we arrive and I'm surprised by the surge of relief I feel when I recognise the hawthorn shelter and the familiar Living area. The group is bigger now because of the hunters but there's easily enough space for everyone to find sleeping and eating positions in the Living. Lively chatter comes from the trees and I could swear that the red squirrels recognise us, happy to see our return.

Straggly branches and leaves have grown in our absence, enclosing the fire pit and choking the sleeping area. It isn't long before Adienna and the other women have woven them into place again, making everything feel right. Snuggling into a fresh bed of leaves, which I've helped to collect, it's such a relief to know the long walk is over.

The following morning, I decide to go for a wash. Returning to the river, I shiver a little. It looks beautiful, bathed in golden sunlight with the sweep of water so enticingly pure, but there is no way I'm going to make the same mistake twice. I fully understand the importance of keeping the water clean. Wandering across to the water pools in the rocks, I splash the dirt away. As I do so, I think about Druantia. I realise that the only time I get important answers from the Elder is when we're on our own; an impossibility during the walk from Fedlimid's home.

The days of long shadows are approaching but it's unlike winter from my future life. The weather is definitely warmer in these times and the changes between seasons marked more by the day length rather than vast differences in temperature. There's a subtle change however, which makes the nights colder and the days fresher. Some of the leaves are turning and falling, but not all of them. I keep trying to see Druantia, but every time I make a move towards her, she's either engrossed in an activity with other people or suddenly not there. Eventually I confide in my friends.

"Why does Druantia keep avoiding me? Every time I try to make an opportunity to see her she disappears."

"Exactly," answers Rhodri. "She will never be there if you look for her, she comes to you in her own time, when she is ready."

This is so annoying but I have to accept it. I've no choice. In the meantime, I spend the days learning different crafts from all the talented people in the Living. One woman, Apirka is really good at making beads from animal bones. The small drill she uses is amazing. Attached to a short stick, the tip of the drill is a finely pointed piece of flint, which delicately digs into the bone. Using a piece of sinew attached to a bow, she pulls the bow backwards and forwards causing the drill to spin. I watch her for ages, marvelling at her skill. Small beads are created, prized by other members of the group. One day I ask Apirka why she spends so long making the beads only to give them away.

"I make them because I love creating something beautiful from the bone. It's a way to respect the animal who has given its life for us. When the beads give pleasure to other people it makes me really happy. What is the point of using them only for me? It is far better to give joy. By sharing we survive well. By being selfish, we survive but without joy or happiness. What is more important?"

I think about that for a bit and decide Apirka is very wise. One Christmas I remember being given a box of chocolates. I really didn't want to share them, so I sneaked them to my room and guzzled the lot. Afterwards, I felt sick but also sad. They hadn't tasted as good as when I'd eaten them before. Previously, I'd shared a similar box with Mum and my aunt's family; we all chose our favourites, talked about them and hoped no-one else would choose the ones we wanted next. For some reason I can't explain, this made them taste better.

As I get to know more people in the Living, I notice that everyone has quite a bit of time on their hands. Once the food is collected and eaten, time is spent in making things, chatting to each other, telling stories or collecting herbs and medicines. Whenever I ask anyone why they do it, they answer as Apirka did, "I enjoy it." Nothing ever seems to be a chore or boring. When one skill has been learnt, a person either spends time refining it, sharing it with other people or trying something different. Amazingly, it all works really well. When everyone is doing exactly what they feel like, every job gets done, with no hardship to anyone. I can't help comparing it with the future when many people seem to dislike their jobs or resent going to work.

Knocking me out of my thoughts, Adara comes running up. "Druantia has had a message, father is ready to travel. The hunters are going to meet him and bring him home." Although her father isn't always here and the whole group looks after the children, I'm very aware of the bond Rhodri and Adara feel for their parents. I give her a big grin. "That's great! It'll be so good to have him back with us again."

Not for the first time, I wonder about the messages. On several occasions people have mentioned messages being sent or received. Initially, I thought nothing of it, but the more I think it over, the more puzzling it seems. There are no mobile phones, no postal service and no way to communicate other than face to face. It's far too dangerous for people to travel alone through the forest; I learnt that the hard way. So how are messages sent? No one ever writes anything down, so it can't be like a carrier pigeon that they used in the 2nd World War.

Another mystery to solve; asking the other two, I get the usual reply. "I'm not sure, but..."

"...Druantia will know, ask her," I finish. "I'd love to ask her but she's never around or there for me to talk to! I give up. I'll not think about meeting her and maybe it will happen."

CHAPTER 23
Reunited

It seems I was right because a few days later Druantia appears, when I'm least expecting to see her. I've been collecting fallen wood and am sitting down to rest on a very inviting tree branch. The Elder walks round the tree to join me.

"What a lovely position you have found, Jenni," she starts. "I approve of your choice of seat." I smile as the Elder sits quietly next to me. Now she's actually here, all the questions I've been collecting in my head fly away. Trying to remember, I look at Druantia and am startled to see her gazing back with an equal intensity. I love being in her presence. It's so right and comfortable; I feel totally at peace.

"The rest of the hunters will be home soon," Druantia continues. "Arthfael has made a wonderful recovery by all accounts. One of the Healers had herbs, which she had traded with a Living from the big marshlands to the east. They have contact with many people who trade from far, far away. Their trades are always worth looking at. It seems that one of these herbs really helped him."

"I am so pleased," I reply. "Did Adienna tell you all about it?"

Druantia looked puzzled, "How would Adienna know? She has been here. No, I heard by message."

This is my chance. One of my questions might be answered.

"How do you send and receive messages?" I ask.

Druantia's wrinkled eyes, full of wisdom, seem to be looking deep, deep inside me before she responds slowly. "Yes, I think I need to tell you this. Do you remember when you treeshifted?"

"Could I forget?" I answer.

"Well, trees are much more than you have already experienced. Have you noticed in a group of trees that there is one who is older and bigger than the rest?" I hadn't but now I think about it, I do recognise that there's always one who seems more important somehow.

"Well, she is the Mother Tree. She sends messages to all the other trees in the area, they all support and help each other to grow, in the same way as we do in the Living."

I nod, fascinated by everything she is saying.

"Under the ground there is a massive system of roots which connect the trees together. Messages are passed along these routes between the trees, they know if one of them is harmed or if one of them needs something. Then, the other trees work together to help them heal or receive the thing it needs."

"How incredible," I whisper.

"Through the years, we have worked very hard to develop trust and love between us and the Tree Spirits. We discuss how to help them and how to enrich the land for all the creatures who share it. The Tree Spirits help and advise us."

"Is it like when I did the treeshifting and met the beautiful Tree Spirit?" I ask.

"It's exactly like that," is her reply. "When we sit

quietly with the tree, the Tree Spirit comes to us and we communicate. Years ago, we went to the trees with a problem. Sometimes we need to pass messages to other humans, but it's too far or too dangerous for us to reach them physically. The trees came up with a solution. We could give them a message, which they send through their system of root connections until it reaches a designated tree near the Living we want to talk to. The Elder has to sit with the tree and then the Tree Spirit will pass on the message."

"What an amazing thing to do! But how do you know if a message is coming?"

"The trees rustle their leaves. The more you live with the trees, the more you begin to understand the different rustles. One sort of tree movement alerts us to any messages coming through. We then go to our special tree, sit very still and communicate with the Tree Spirit."

"I don't understand how the Tree Spirits know who the message is for."

"Every Living has an Elder who is the main tree communicator. When they become initiated into that role, they are given a name by the Tree Spirit, which helps them to be identified. All the tree communicators are aware of each other's names, so if we are sending a message, we tell the trees who it is for and they pass it to that person."

"But when I was with the hunters there wasn't an Elder in the group."

"No, but when you ran off, they were near another Living. I sent the message to all the Elders in the area to look out for you and to inform the hunters to do the same. Luckily people from that Living were able to find our hunters who then looked out for you." I start to feel guilty again for all the trouble I've caused.

At that moment the leaves start rustling. Druantia glances across with a twinkle in her eye. "Now you will see how we receive and send messages." She moves across to a nearby tree and sits against it. Closing her eyes, she's soon as still as the trunk behind her. I watch as Druantia's features relax. I reckon this is going to take some time, so I slide off the branch and lean back against another tree. The rustling has stopped so I gaze up at the sky, which is a deep blue, filtered by the brilliant green, orange and gold lacing of the leaves. Feeling better, a peaceful calm spreads through me.

After a while, Druantia opens her eyes again.

"That was a message from the next Living to ours. The hunters stayed with them last night, so they will be here tomorrow. We need to prepare for their return."

Our chat is over. Druantia hurries off to share the news. I suppose that's something which never changes, people through the centuries always prepare for their loved ones returning with care and excitement.

With the return of Arthfael and the hunters comes another supply of meat. They used their journey to collect food for everyone. It's incredible how everyone thinks and and lives for the whole group, with no selfishness. Eager hands help to prepare the feast to celebrate Arthfael's safe return and the hunters' good fortune. My friends are overjoyed to see their father again. Adara flings herself on him and although the well-built man flinches a little when she catches his sore side, he hides it well and hugs her back. Rhodri grins at him, beaming from ear to ear.

CHAPTER 24
Red Spikes and Green Waves

When the hunters are around, the squirrels don't seem so friendly. I ask Rhodri about this.
"Oh it's because they kill. Even though they do it with respect and only for food, the other creatures can sense it, so they don't trust them. That's why some people of the Living choose not to hunt and work with the animals to gather food instead. We need a mixture of leaves, berries and nuts as well as meat, so each person chooses to gather food in the way which suits them best."

"I don't know why you bother with her, she knows so little," sneers a voice behind us. Even before I turn, I know the pinched face of Froni will be glaring at me.
"Go away," retorts Rhodri, "why can't you leave her alone?"
"Oooh and who's going to make me?" challenges the girl.
"Don't listen to her," Adara says, "come on Jenni, let's go and collect nuts."
Froni isn't going to let it go. "Ignoring me are you? How does that help us all work together as a group? That's not fitting in with our Living's agreements. I'd better go and tell Druantia about this, I wonder what she'll say. She won't be happy to hear the odd one out is causing problems again," she smirks in my direction.

That girl always seems to touch a raw nerve. It's

so unfair. I can feel my face flaring red. "Shut up and go away!" I advance on Froni, maddened with anger. Years of nasty comments from others boil inside. "What's your problem? Why are you so horrid? What have I done? I didn't ask to come here. It happened. I can't change it, believe you me I have tried, but I can't. Just go away and leave me alone!"

My voice gets louder and louder. Squirrels scatter across branches above, while many people from the Living gradually gather around us, unused to hearing raised voices. Froni stands rooted to the spot, staring at me as I spit venom. She looks shocked at my anger. Suddenly she notices the others watching. Her face takes on a defiant look, her eyes narrow and she yells back at me, "Well, at least I don't harm our precious water supply or lead my friends into danger by the Big Water. No wonder you don't have any friends where you come from, they must be too scared you'll hurt them in some way."

All I can see are 'red spikes' shooting out around my head. They blind me, as I run at Froni. Throwing myself on her, I lose all control. My arms and legs seem to be flying in every direction, kicking and scratching, trying to harm her in any way I can.

Suddenly, I feel strong arms restraining me, dragging me away.

"Let me go!" I yell. "She deserves it!"

As I'm being pulled , I catch a glimpse of Rhodri's face in the crowd, shaken and shocked. "Come away, or you will regret it," the voice of the strong arms says. I struggle and kick against my captor, panic rising. Someone touches my head. Instantly, blackness swirls through my mind and I fall into a deep sleep.

Sometime later, I awake in the original bower of trees where I'd been put on my arrival. Blinking, I try to get my thoughts together. What happened? Slowly I recall it all and my face burns with shame. I've never behaved like that with another human. How did I get so out of control? With horror, I remember the look on Rhodri's face and squirm with embarrassment. Why oh why, did I let that girl get to me?

I turn my head and see Druantia. That makes it even worse. Her kind and gentle behaviour is so good, it makes me look five times nastier. A grim worm of self-hate grows inside, filling me with a dull greyness. Why do I always mess everything up? Turning away, silent tears pour down my face.

"Why are you crying?" asks the wise woman. I should know better than to try and hide from Druantia.

"I've made such a mess of everything since I came here. I've put you and my friends in danger, I've polluted the beautiful pure water, which everyone relies on and finally I have lost my temper and attacked Froni.I didn't know I had that much strength. Is she alright? Did I hurt her badly? I feel so terrible. You must all think I'm so horrible. Just let me go back to the future and then you can all forget about me. I wish I had never come here."

"First of all Froni is fine; shocked and stunned but she's okay. Secondly what makes you think you

know our thoughts? Are you a mind reader?"
"Well no, but it's obvious isn't it? I behaved really badly; no one else has attacked anyone like that since I came here. Your whole community relies on people getting on with each other and living together for the good of everyone."
"Are you forgetting there was someone else involved here? A person who provoked you until you lost your temper?" replies Druantia.
"Well no, but what I did was beyond what she'd done. She only taunted me with words." I pause for a moment then it all comes flooding out, "It's gone on since I arrived. She never liked me. She was the one who stuffed moss into my mouth and mocked me so that I ended up in the river. She has kept making nasty little comments, always finding a chance to hurt me. Most of all she made me feel like I do in the future. There, I am left out of everything; no one wants me to be their friend. It was so special here. I finally had real friends and was part of a group." The tears start to fall again but I don't bother trying to hide them. There's no point.
"Do you think that maybe Froni was feeling a little like you did in the future? She was the one alone and isolated. She felt left out of the group. Had you ever thought about what it was like before you came?"
"Was she their friend?" I ask.
"She was starting to build a friendship with Adara. It had taken her a long time after her mother was killed and her father left. She quietly resented Adara and Rhodri. Her mother had secretly told

her that her unhappiness was because of Adienna and that she should avoid the whole family." Druantia looks sad. "It is easier to help a child change than a grown woman. If only we had seen the unhappiness in her mother before it was too late. Maybe some of that was my fault." A deep sigh comes from her mouth. "Since her mother died, all the other women in the Living have been helping Froni to change her opinions and to start to build friendships with the children of Adienna. Adara is such an easy going, loving and caring girl. It wasn't hard for her to start to make a connection with Froni and to break down the years of resentment. Then you came along with all the excitement of being from somewhere different and she felt pushed out. Like you in the future, she cut herself off from everyone and turned in on herself."

"So is that why she was so mean? She was jealous?"

"Of course she was. It is a very natural emotion but it can do a lot of harm. In our close ways of living we cannot allow jealousy to come and harm our community. That's why I feel so sad to have missed the signs in Froni's mother. We have to work together or nothing works. Both of you have been harmed and hurt. You will now see how we change that." Druantia walks from the bower, indicating I should follow.

Outside, a group of people have formed a circle. In the middle is Froni. Her expression is unreadable. A feeling that something terrible is about to happen sticks in my belly and won't go away.

"What will happen to her?" I ask Druantia in a whisper.
"Wait and see. Trust," is the reply.

As the Elder joins the group, pulling me with her, the group starts to sing. Each individual person sings their own melody, but as usual each voice harmonises with every other. However, this time something is different. They are singing with words. I listen carefully and pick some out. Every person is singing to Froni about how they love her, care for her and want her to be happy.

With a lurch of my stomach, I suddenly realised I'm expected to join in. This can't be happening. It's just too hard. How can they expect me to do this? I can't sing unless I feel the truth of what I am singing. How can I pretend to like her? With a deep sigh I look at Froni. I try really hard not to see the mean, unpleasant person who taunted me, but a sad, lonely, little girl who's lost her mother and only wants friends. The swelling of the music all around helps and after a long while, I finally start to sing in a very quiet voice. There's no way I can sing that I love her, so I start by singing that I care for her. I can just about manage that.

Surprisingly, as I sing, I slowly begin to feel as if I really do care. I can actually see the waves of love flooding through Froni. 'Swathes of green in every shade' flow around her, bathing her in warmth and love as every person in the group sends her their highest emotion.

As we watch, a change starts to happen to Froni. The constant scowl is replaced and she starts to sob. Tears flow down her little face and she sits hunched on the ground. The singing intensifies and I finally begin to feel real compassion for the girl. It must be so hard to be in the middle of that circle with all those people looking at you and giving you all this attention. Finally, Froni stands up. She seems taller and straighter than she'd been before, while an unusual smile starts to filter into the corners of her mouth.

By this time I'm singing as hard as anyone else. I close my eyes for a while to help me to concentrate on the sound and when I open them I see that Froni has started to move around the circle. She's going to each person and giving them a hug. Froni reaches Adara who gives her a big hug back, then Rhodri. She's slowly moving round, edging closer. Butterflies start to go mad in my tummy. What will happen when she gets to me? I concentrate on trying to think caring thoughts, blocking out the nasty stuff. Froni is at Druantia now. The Elder holds her and pours so much love into her that I can feel the waves enveloping me as well.

Oh no, it's my turn. I look up and into Froni's eyes. A reflection of my own pain flits across them before it's replaced with hope. "I am sorry," whispers Froni.

"So am I," I reply and I'm surprised to realise that I really mean it.

Suddenly our arms are around each other and I'm awash in 'green waves of love' as the whole group supports us.

Froni moves back into the middle of the circle, holding my hand and bringing me with her. Feeling better and happier than ever, I grin round at the group of people who've taken me to their hearts and smile at the girl who's been my nemesis for so long. The singing dies down and Druantia speaks.

"Now you two have seen and understood why you didn't get along, you need to be kind and work together, not against each other. You are both loved and with love, there is always enough to go around, it is never-ending. Remember this day, if either of you ever think of slipping away from your higher feelings. Love heals all. Now, go peacefully about your day."

CHAPTER 25
Questions and Answers

The circle breaks up and I smile at Froni.
"Why don't we go and sit with Adara and Rhodri to eat our food?" She gives me a hesitant smile and joins us. As I eat, I think about my behaviour in the twenty first century. Do I push others away? Have I sometimes made hurtful remarks to other children when I've felt rejected? I probably have. I wonder if others look on me as I used to look at Froni? It's not a very nice feeling, so I decide to try and be more pleasant when I return to the future.

The days pass, the nights are getting longer and the friendship between all four of us grows and blossoms. No one refers to the past; we simply get on with enjoying each other's company. Froni seems a changed person. She's much happier and smiling more. No one's left out, if Adara is chatting to Froni, then I spend time with Rhodri or sometimes brother and sister are involved in an activitiy, so Froni and I link up. Soon it's hard to remember that Froni hasn't always been a part of our group.

One day I'm sitting in a clearing, collecting nuts from a squirrel when Druantia appears.
"You have really learnt our ways now," smiles the Elder.
"I'm glad you think so," I answer.
"It is time for me to start explaining a few things," starts Druantia.

"Before long you will have to return to the future. I'm not sure if you will ever get back here and if you don't, there are certain things you need to know." The joy at finally finding Druantia is ready to speak, is tinged by a dreadful feeling of loss. I will have to leave Adara, Rhodri and even Froni behind. As if she can read my mind, Druantia explains, "Don't regret your friends here. You will find them again in different people."
"I don't understand."
"You will one day," she replies, sounding annoyingly like my mum. "Now, before I answer your questions would you answer some of mine?"
I'm flattered that Druantia wants to ask me something and quickly nod. "Why do you feel so left out and alone in the future?" That wasn't quite what I was expecting and don't really want to answer. I think about it for a while. Druantia waits patiently. Maybe it would help to talk about my past hurt. I feel so far away now, it's a bit easier.
"Well," I start, "I always blamed my mum. She didn't let us have a television."
"Please can you explain what that is?" Druantia asks.
How do I explain a telly to someone who knows nothing of modern life?
"It's a sort of magic box which sits in the corner of everyone's Living. It has pictures and sounds telling people what is happening in other places on the Earth. A lot of the time it also has made up stories about people and animals."
"Who makes these pictures come into the box and how do they do it?"

"I don't really know," I reply. "I've never really thought about it. I suppose it's the people who make the programme...the stories. Lots of different people make them but I think they have to be checked before they are shown. My mum doesn't like it because she says it is mind control, telling everyone how to think and what to talk about, but I feel really left out because everyone else discusses the stories they have seen on it and I haven't."

"How many people are in your Living?"

"There's my mum and me."

"That's a very small Living. Are all the Livings the same?"

"Well, it's not really like a Living. We all belong to one massive Living, which is called a town."

"How many people live in this 'town'?"

"I don't know, many more than the Gathering, maybe as many Gatherings as I have fingers." Druantia rolled her eyes at the thought of so many people in one Living.

She asks, "So, why did you call your group a Living?"

"I didn't know what else to call it. Maybe it would be better to call it a family group, like Adienna, Rhodri, Adara and Arthfael are a family group. Each family group lives in their own building called a house. Each house has its own television."

"This is much for me to think about. So do all the people watch this television?"

"Most people, yes. There are also computers, which is sort of like the television but you connect with it more. Oh dear, this is really complicated. It's so hard to explain."

"I think we need to focus on one thing at a time. You say you have never had this television in your house?"
"No," I pull a face. "It's so unfair."
"That is the reason, my little friend, why you came here."
Shocked, I look up at Druantia. "What do you mean?"
"I mean that your mind is very strong and free. I don't know what stories are told on this box but stories are very powerful. They tell of where we have come from, they tell of ways to behave, they tell of how to keep a balance."
"The stories other children talk about don't appear to do that," I respond. "It mainly seems to be about people falling out with each other, killing each other and arguing. A lot of the news about other people around the world is the same," I add.
"I'm not surprised your mum doesn't allow it. She sounds like a very wise woman," counters Druantia. No one has ever called my mum wise before. I'm stunned.
Druantia suddenly changes the conversation. "Now, what do you want to know from me?" My mind goes blank. "Think, think," I tell myself. "Here's your chance, what do you want to know?" In a flash it comes back to me, the question I'd been longing to ask.
"Could you explain, please, what happened when we were walking to Fedlimid's Living?"
"Now you have explained something that was puzzling me, I can answer your question. I was wondering why you and no one else from your

future has come through. One explanation, although I am not convinced it is the whole reason, is that you are not mind controlled like many of the future people are. As a result, your mind is able to accept and believe in things, which other people will not."

"That's true," I think. "I'm sure many people don't live in their imaginations like I do." Aloud I say, "I doubt many people would stand by a tree and try to make themselves invisible or believe they had travelled back in time."

"Exactly, so your mind is very strong and able to see what many other people can't. Your mind is open. You have much to thank your mother for."

I'd never thought I would hear those words but yes, I suppose I do.

"But what happened, on that day?"

"What were you thinking?"

"I was wondering about the paths we were walking and if they eventually would become roads for cars to drive on."

"I think I had a glimpse of these things called cars. Are they loud and noisy and smelly? Do they move very, very fast?"

"Yes, they do," I reply. "How did you get to see them?"

"Your mind created a link with the future through your imagination and of course your memories of that Time. This caused you to start to slip back. In this time you started to fade, which was when Rhodri called out. I realised you would arrive in the future in the same position on the Earth. That could have been very dangerous. Anything could have been there. A gorge could have formed, a waterfall, or as you discovered it was a path, but for these things you call cars."

"They are very dangerous," I answer. "If I had walked out in front of them, I would have been killed; luckily you managed to stop me."

"That really would have been terrible," the Elder replies. "I don't know how that would work with the time slip as well."

"But how could you travel through time and grab me?"

"I, also, have many powers in my mind developed through many years of training. We have a strong connection, you and I. I don't know why or how, but we do. I felt it when you first came through and I healed you. Maybe it was the healing. Maybe it is something else. Who knows? One day it will be clear to me. For now, all I understand is that we are connected."

"Is that why I can only understand everyone when you are around?" I ask.

"I think it is very likely," the Elder responds. "As we worked out before, water seems to cut off your link with me and it isn't reconnected until we are near each other again. I seem to be acting as a translator. This has never happened to me before and I am learning as you learn."

Suddenly she changes her tone. "I think that is enough talking for now. Go and join your friends. Enjoy your last moons together. When the long shadows become shorter and we don't eat meat, the time will come for your attempt to return to the future. I discussed you with other wise Elders

at the Gathering. We came to an idea about how you can go home. They have suggested something involving treeshifting, which I think will work but we have to wait and see. However, no one can treeshift when they have eaten meat; the body becomes denser which makes it harder to transform. To blend with the tree energy, we need to only eat products from the tree. So, until we return to our new shoots food, it can't be tried."
As she finishes speaking, I watch her fade away, "I must ask her how she does that," is my last thought before entering the Living space.

CHAPTER 26
Back to the Present

The moons of the long shadow days herald the longest night and a large fire is lit for warmth. It reminds me of the sun's fire and the life it gives to everything. Many stories are told by the Elders of times gone by, of ways to live in balance and warnings of what could happen if we forget to live carefully. I love all the stories and treasure them, realising that my time with the people I've grown to love is getting shorter.

Through the long shadow months Druantia instructs me on many things, particularly on how to control my emotions and thoughts. I also learn how Druantia can fade and reappear where and when she wants. "It's a bit like you did, when you went back into the future," states the Elder. "I imagine every tiny part of my being in a place where I want to be. Then I see myself there. I can only manage to do it across short distances but it is very useful." I have a go in private when no one else is around but no matter how hard I try, I can't do it. I realise it must have taken Druantia many, many years to achieve and isn't something that can happen instantly.

I'm becoming more and more aware that this blissful time isn't going to last forever. Druantia keeps trying to prepare me, reminding me that when the new shoots come, the time to return will be near. I keep pushing it to the back of my mind, enjoying my friends' company. They too glance at me now and again, I'm sure they are also feeling the same.

The Elder sees and understands. All too soon, the long shadows start to shorten, new shoots appear, plant growth surges and the hunters leave to start collecting food for the Gathering. The signs are there and I notice them.

One day, my friends have gone to gather food but I'm not feeling very hungry. I sit with my back to my favourite tree, enjoying the soft green love as we exchange feelings. "I wonder if I will be able to do this when I return?" I muse.

"Try it and see," responds the Tree Spirit.

Druantia suddenly does one of her appearing acts."I have something very special to reveal to you. It is not something that many people know about or understand. The only reason I am showing you is because you are from another Time. Normally it is only the Elders who know of this. I have consulted the other Elders and they agree I can take you but on one condition; that you keep this knowledge to yourself."

Very intrigued, I agree and followed my mentor as we walk quite a distance from the Living Space. Soon we arrive at a small cave tucked into an overhang of rock. Above the overhang, nothing grows on the rocky surface. It is a rare, clear space in the normally dense forest. In the middle of the rocky outcrop is a tall, straight stick, supported and held by many rocks and stones, carefully wedging the stick in place. Druantia indicates that I should come closer.

"Come with me." Together we walk up the rocky incline, giving her my arm when she needs it for support. As we reach the top, I notice that the rock has many lines of different colour in it. The older woman notices my gaze.
"When the shadow from the stick reaches this line," she points to a deep striation in the rock, "I know it is time to start the walk to the Gathering." I sense I'm being shown something very precious and important to the Elder. I listen respectfully. "When you first arrived, I knew it was a special day," explains Druantia. "I came up here and noted where the shadow fell." With great care she indicates a point where one line in the rock crossed another. "Here." She touches the point gently. "As you can see, the shadows are nearly there. When they are lined up exactly as they were, it will be time for you to leave."

I look at the stick, so simple yet so important in my life. Part of me wants to tear the stick out, so I'll never have to return. Another part of me knows that I would never do that. Respect for Druantia and love for Mum prevents me. I've always known I'll have to return and face my life as it was. Maybe, things can be different now? I hope so. Looking carefully at the stick I reckon I've probably got only a few days left.

On returning to my friends, I'm determined to concentrate on making the last days perfect.
One fresh morning, the sun is filtering through the leaves, dewdrops are sparkling on the mossy stones and I'm drinking in the happiness. "Could it ever get better than this?" I think. As if reading

my thoughts, Druantia appears. Behind her walk Adienna and Cara. Cara is carrying a bundle. The Elder speaks first. "Today it seems it is the time for you to leave."

I can feel my face fall. "So soon?" I whisper. "These last days have gone so quickly."

"I am sorry but yes. If you stay longer I cannot guarantee you will ever return. I have also had messages from the Tree Spirits who told me the time is right. You cannot delay."

"Can I at least say goodbye to my friends?"

"Of course, but before you make your farewells, Cara and Adienna have something for you."

Cara steps forward and I see that she's holding out my jeans and T-shirt. "I rain washed them for you, then Druantia found somewhere to keep them. We realised you would need to return in the clothes of your Time. Here you are." I hold them to my face. A strong smell of herbs and the forest lingers around them. I sniff deeply, wanting to preserve the smell forever.

It feels very strange to be putting on my tight, clingy jeans and T-shirt after the looseness of my beautiful leaf dress. Sadly, I hand it back to Cara. "Thank you for the best gift I was ever given," I whisper as I give her a big hug. I turn to Adienna, "Thank you for teaching me how to work with the animals, I shall never forget you." Blue eyes smile as a wave of love sweeps through me.

"Hurry child," Druantia prompts, "Time is passing. You need to be at the tree ready to return very soon."

"Have I still time to see my friends?"

"Yes, but not long, the shadows are moving."

With a heavy feeling inside I hurry off to find Adara, Rhodri and Froni. They know as soon as they see me. Adara runs to me and flings her arms around my neck. "I don't know what to say," she sobs. "Will we ever see you again?"

I fight to hold back the tears. "I really don't know. All I do know is that I will try."

Rhodri moves forward next and I step into his arms. The hug is long and I feel my pain echoed in his. Neither of us say anything until we part.

"I'll never forget you my treeshifter," he whispers.

"You will always be in my heart," I whisper back.

Choking on my tears, I move on to Froni who's standing back a little.

"Well you've got what you finally wished for when I first arrived!" I joke through the mist of water filling my eyes.

"I never thought I'd say this but that is the last thing I wish for now," she replies. "You have given me so much. I have learnt to love."

"Me too," I whisper back. "Thank you."

"We need to hurry," interrupts Druantia, the sun is almost in the exact position. We need to try with everything in the right place." Throwing my friends a last sad glance I hurry after Druantia. It's not long before we are by the tree I first travelled through.

"Quickly now," she says, "position yourself and think into your treeshifting mind, as I have taught you to."

I hurry into position, trying to recall all the practice I've gone through during the preceding months, as I place my mind at one with the tree. Green light floods through, swirling shades of the colour invade every sense, as I'm taken up in the arms of the Tree Spirit. A superb feeling of well-being swims around my body and I lose myself in the moment, as a voice in my head calms me and tells me I'm safe. The sensation of buzzing fills every part of me as more and more green swirls in and around. Time loses all meaning.

Suddenly, I am aware of solid ground beneath my feet. This is it. I try not to think of what will happen if I haven't returned to my own Time.

Gingerly, I open my eyes. There is the familiar path, the wall and the sheep grazing in the field beyond. Behind me, my favourite tree seems to be glowing with a very strong, greenish tinge. As I watch, it begins to fade and the colours around me come into perspective. They look very jaded and lifeless compared with the landscape with which I've become so familiar. With a sigh of relief, I realise that Druantia and the Tree Spirits have done it. I'm back.

In fact, I feel very happy to be home. Racing along the path, I rush along the road and down the steep slope until I reach our cottage. Bursting through the door, I see Mum standing by the sink, looking sad and tired. With an overwhelming feeling of love, I rush in and hug her so hard, she nearly falls.

"What's brought this change on?" her mum asks with a surprised smile. "A short while ago you were storming out, hating everything I stood for."

"Oh mum, you have no idea how much I love you

and all you have done for me," I answer. My mum looks as if she's wondering whether she's heard right. She looks at me closely. I smile back. That seems to put her into a greater shock. She doesn't say anything though. A big beam crosses her face and she looks happier than she has in months.

Later that night as I snuggle down in my lovely soft bed, I think about the next day at school. Tomorrow I will try out all the things I've learnt from Druantia. It probably won't happen overnight, but I know now how to give out love, change attitudes and start to build friendships. I'll gradually do it, I know I will.

As I drift off to sleep, a thought hits me and I sit bolt upright. Oh no! In all the hurry to treeshift at the right time, I didn't say goodbye to Druantia. Overwhelming sadness fills me at not having said my farewells to the woman I so greatly admire, love and respect. 'Clouds of grey' swirl around and all the euphoria of my return starts to fade. Then a little voice in my head makes itself heard, "Maybe you didn't say goodbye because you will see her another time?"

Immediately, I don't feel quite so sad and a 'little swirl of green' drifts around my head. With the beginning of a smile on my face, I doze off, hopeful that one day we will meet again.

EPILOGUE

I sit under the spindly beech tree. Nothing has changed. Kenzo and his cronies fly passed, arms and coats flying, "Jerky Jenni, Jerky Jenni!" On the benches Zari and Mina giggle together about some massively important secret.

But something has changed. I don't care anymore. I bend my head and sense the lingering smell of forest on my T-shirt. A small smile curves across my lips. Green waves of love swirl between me and the sad little tree. I feel delicate tendrils reaching out and a soft caress across my back, as the neglected Tree Spirit tentatively wakes up.

"I will protect you," I whisper and at that moment I know what I need to do. In whatever way I can, in small ways and maybe big ways, I will protect and look after the trees, starting with this one.

All of a sudden, a little face appears beside me. Brown eyes framed by bouncy curls look up at me. "Do you like this beech tree as well?" the girl asks. I'm completely taken aback. My old self would have been dismissive of a younger child, but this girl looks so like Adara. I focus all my attention on her.

"I do actually. She's a very special tree and we need to look after her. Would you help me?"

"Oh yes!" the child responds eagerly. She grins up at me, as I feel a reflection of that grin beaming across my own face.

On the bench Zari and Mina look up. I catch

snatches of their conversation. “That strange girl, Jenni is actually smiling, it transforms her sulky face.”
“Yeh, there’s something different about her today, something I can’t say. She has a sort of glow around her, which make her look a bit better than normal.” Then Zari says something in a lower voice and they both giggle. As they watch, Jonti wanders across to us. Immediately the smiles are wiped off their faces and I can see them leaning forward trying to hear what he is saying.

Brown eyes sparkling with amusement, he approaches us sitting by the beech tree. “Hello little sis, have you got yourself a new friend? My name’s Jonti by the way.”

As he extends his hand I feel a shock of recognition. Those eyes, no, they can’t be... Trying to stop myself from flinging my arms out to give him a big hug, I slowly take the proffered hand. An echo of Rhodri’s cheeky grin suffuses Jonti’s face. Suddenly, I decide that school isn’t so bad after all.

Appendix

Although this story is fictional, I thoroughly researched the historical background to inform my writing about the Mesolithic period, about which little is known in comparison to the later, Neolithic time.

The Mesolithic period is from the last Ice Age, about 11,600 years ago to 6,000 years ago (9,600-4,000 B.C.) From what I have read, the climate seems to have been warmer. Britain was attached to mainland Europe by a low-lying marshy area, which is nowadays referred to as Doggerland (now under the North Sea). In the book I refer to the marshy lands to the east, which is this area. During those five thousand years (which is more than double the time from the Romans to present day) people seemed to have lived as hunters and gatherers.

Animal bones found have shown that deer, aurochs, elk, and wild boar lived at this time, as did red squirrels, wolves and many bird species. Excavations at Star Carr near Scarborough have shown remains of these creatures. The use of shellfish and hazelnuts were discovered at an excavation in Howick, Northumberland, which has revealed a roundhouse by the sea. This is the basis for the part of the story set in Fedlimid's village, although I envisioned this being on the south coast. Charred plant remains found on Mesolithic sites in Scotland and elsewhere in Britain have included crab apple and pear pips, haw berry stones, hazelnut shells and the roots of Lesser Celandine, which would be a little like very small potatoes.

I was fascinated to read about Blick Mead in the area of Stonehenge, where, a spring of water has been found and a site which historians believe once held a seasonal lake, plus a rare Mesolithic building has been discovered; which all suggests to archaeologists that there was a settlement there prior to the famous stone circle's construction. This is where I set the Gathering. Archaeologists have discovered the remains of many cooked aurochs, which suggests that large gatherings were held here, aurochs being in plentiful supply to feed everyone. There have also been many flint tools discovered in a layer of silt at this site; many more than anywhere else in the entire region, including a slate, which is only found in North Wales. All of these are reasons to speculate that many people from all across Britain gathered at this spot in Mesolithic times.

The pink flint mentioned in the story is totally unique to the area and caused by algae, *Hildenbrandia rivularis*, which grows because of dappled light and the unusually warm spring water in the area. This is maybe another reason why the area became a place of gatherings.

For more detailed explanation explore the following links:
http://www.archaeology.co.uk/articles/features/vespasians-camp-cradle-of-stonehenge.htm

https://www.buckingham.ac.uk/research/hri/fellows/jacques

http://www.buckingham.ac.uk/contact-us/information-for-the-media/press-releases/stonehenge-dig-latest-findings/

The idea for the storyteller's tale at the Gathering was suggested to me when I read about the excavations of the Bosnian Pyramids. There are two conflicting views about the ongoing excavations there. One is that it is a complete sham, the other that they are the remains of three massive pyramids, now disguised as hills. It is claimed that there are ice age deposits on the northern slopes of the supposed pyramids, to suggest they predate the ice age. It is also claimed that there is concrete on the site, which is thousands of years old. Apparently, inside these pyramids, the air is fresh and rejuvenating. I haven't been there myself and cannot verify these statements. However, I took the liberty of an author's license for the ideas to fire my imagination and create the tale of how people survived the ice age and emerged into a new world wanting to work in harmony with their environment.

In the story told by the storyteller, he refers to a previous civilisation, which was destroyed by the Ice Age. The concept that there have been other highly civilised societies on this planet, prior to this present one, is held in many different cultures and stories around the world. In our own culture there is the legend of Atlantis. The Hopi in North America tell of there being three worlds prior to this one. Each was destroyed when men became out of balance with nature; the first being destroyed by fire from volcanic activity, the second by the ice age and the third by water (other flood legends also run through many cultures through the world). We are now in the fourth age. These were the ideas that prompted the story.

Giants are referred to in many of our traditional stories, sometimes as benign, sometimes as bad. Apparently skeletons of giants have been found in many different places around the world, there are statues of giant people in ancient cultures and giants are referred to in the Bible, which some people claim has a basis in historical fact. I always go on the idea that there is 'no smoke without fire'. If giants had never existed then why would humans have the concept of them? It would explain many things about the mysteries of the past. In Greek and other legends, giants are often linked with the God's people from the sky, who could also be people from the stars. Who knows? Again I have taken creative liberties with the idea and woven them into the story.

The chewing gum referred to in the story is birch bark tar. Birch bark tar has been used in northern Europe as far back as 80,000 years. It was found on a Neanderthal spear point, with a thumbprint. Pieces of chewed birch bark tar with human teeth marks go back as far as 11,000 years.

If you want more information explore this link:

http://www.primitiveways.com/birch_bark_tar.html

Acknowledgements

Firstly, I thank The Promoting Yorkshire Authors group. Their combined support, courses, advice and sharing of knowledge has been phenomenal, guiding me through the mystifying maze of publishing and marketing. I believe it is the new way of working in business; collaboration and sharing and it certainly seems to work.

Harry J Davies needs a massive thank you for his fabulous artwork in designing the cover, and Sara Simpson for the brilliant layout of the text on the cover. Also thanks to Joey Wright for his design work on the website which links with the book.

I also thank Professor David Jacques and his team from Buckingham University for their inspiring work at Blick Mead, which provided the background information for the chapter on the Gathering and fed into the educational materials on the website.

Thank you to my wonderful friend Sandra Macleod who has been there for me every step of the way, reading my initial drafts, making suggestions to improve them and giving me tea and sympathy at every stage.

Many thanks to my beautiful young friend Lola who was my first child reader; her total belief in my writing gave me confidence to continue, while her invaluable comments helped me to make tweaks to the story that rounded it off perfectly.

Many thanks to all my Beta Readers; Robin Wyeth and Mel Scott, Lola Howard-Simpson, Jago Thoma-Jones

Rachel Low, Sandra Macleod and Jo Remington, for their willingness to read it and write their comments about **A Tree in Tree.**

Can I also thank Bev Davies, Pat Williams, Heather Colbran, Lauren Reed and Kay Handoll and the children in classes 3 and 5/6 (2018) at Castle Hill School for reading or listening to the different drafts and giving their invaluable feedback,

Thanks to Wendy Yorke and Susan Mears Agency for directing me towards the professional approach to publishing and taking me through the early stages.

Thank you to my amazing friends Jan Lee, Catherine Horton and Rachel Coyle who suggested writing the book in the first place through our wonderful meditation sessions.

Thanks to the organisers of the 2019 Wells Literary Festival who saw the potential in the book and shortlisted it for a Children's Author prize and the judge, Gill Lewis, for her valuable feedback.

Finally, I thank all the contributors from various Internet sources who fed into the research for the book, the amazing people whom I have met during my life who have inspired me, and my supportive husband and son who have put up with the hours I spent whiling away on the computer.

If you have enjoyed this book, it would be wonderful if you could plant a tree in a place where it can grow freely and with space to mature safely.

Lightning Source UK Ltd.
Milton Keynes UK
UKHW041248300921
391375UK00004B/96